K. A. Last
kalast@kalastbooks.com.au
www.kalastbooks.com.au

ISBN: 978-0-6480257-9-5

Formatting and cover design © KILA Designs www.kiladesigns.com.au

ELLA
AND ASH

K. A. LAST

www.kalastbooks.com.au

Books by K. A. Last

YA Fantasy Fiction
Sacrifice – A Fall For Me Prequel
Fall For Me (The Tate Chronicles, #1)
Fight For Me (The Tate Chronicles, #2)
Die For Me (The Tate Chronicles, #3)
Immagica
The Lovely Dark
Ella and Ash (Happily Ever After, #1)
Chasing Neve (Happily Ever After, #2)
False Princess (Happily Ever After, #3)
Dance of Wishes (Happily Ever After, #4)
Winter Flame (Happily Ever After, #5)

YA Contemporary Fiction
Something (All the Things: part one)
Nothing (All the Things: part two)
Everything (All the Things: part three)
The Other Side of Me (All the Things: part four)

Non-fiction
A Novel Idea! Colouring Journal for Writers
A Novel Idea Workbook for Writers

To everyone still looking for their happily ever after,
I hope you find it.

1

The coarse rock is cool beneath my hand as I press my palm to the headstone of my mother's grave. I close my eyes, and listen to the rustle of leaves, jostled by the breeze wafting through the weeping willow that grows here. I planted it myself when Mother died three years ago, to watch over and protect her. The tree is our connection, and through it I feel as though she is right here with me.

I open my eyes, and run my finger over the gold lettering etched into the headstone.

"How are you today?" I ask, kneeling on the grass.

There's no answer. None that I can hear anyway.

She usually speaks to me in different ways. Through the earth, and the plants, and the animals. Today, the majestic willow tree sways gently, and I take it as a sign all is well with her.

"I've not had such a great time," I say. "Anna and Drew are up to their usual tricks. And I don't *want* to complain, but it's so hard to be nice to them. They wouldn't let me into the house at all the other day. Lady Roche didn't allow me to have dinner. She said I'd slacked off on my chores. But I couldn't do them because I couldn't get inside."

The grass at the base of my mother's grave tickles my knees, and I readjust my position so I'm sitting cross-legged in front of her. I run my fingers over the soft blades, and watch them move at my touch.

"I won't complain anymore," I continue. "I'm sure you don't really want to hear how badly they treat me. It's just … some days are much harder than others."

My eyes grow hot, and I get to my feet. I always cry when I come to see my mother. It's the only place where I'm able to really be myself, and not worry about anyone looking or seeing or judging me. I step around the headstone and go towards the willow tree, part the weeping branches, then place my palm against its rough bark.

The tree sighs under my touch, and tears spill from my eyes, falling on the earth at the base of the trunk. The tendrils of leaves sway around me as light from my magic seeps out of the ground, coiling in wispy lines around the tree, before spreading out to every branch, feeding it and helping it grow.

The pendant around my neck glows the same azure blue as my magic, and I close my eyes as my last tear falls to water the tree. Turning my face upwards, I open my eyes again and gaze at the shroud of magic I've created. I'm protected inside its bubble as it drips from the branches and leaves. The willow grows visibly taller, and the branches extend.

I reach out with my mind and snag a wispy blue trail of magic, twisting it gently until it forms the shape of a swallow. The little bird chirps, swooping from branch to branch, flitting through the curtain of leaves. I giggle, my tears forgotten, then create two more birds as companions. I hold up my arm where the three of them alight.

"Would you be so kind, and keep me company for a bit?" I ask.

The birds chirp in unison, then dart in and out of the leafy curtain before perching high in the tree.

"That's a pretty neat trick," a voice says.

The smile falls from my face.

Someone's here. Have they seen my magic?

I part the willow tree's curtain. A boy stands in the open, his head tilted back, watching my birds as they fly in and out of the willow. I wave my hand, and my magic dissipates. The birds dissolve and disappear. Leaves from the willow flutter to the ground.

"You startled me." I step away from the tree, not wanting this boy, whoever he is, to come any closer to it.

He doesn't reply. He just stands there with a funny little smirk on his face. His lips curl up ever so slightly, more so on one side. I get a strong feeling that I know him from somewhere, but I'm sure we've never formally met. He's smartly dressed, wearing pressed navy trousers and a crisp white shirt. The boy puts his hands in his pockets, and rocks back and forth on his heels. I study him, trying to remember where I've seen him before.

"I'm sure you know who I am," the boy says in a rather confident voice. "I'm Ashwin Chethan."

My mouth drops open, but I quickly close it.

Ashwin Chethan.

No wonder he looks familiar. And no wonder he's standing there in all his self-assured glory. He's the son of the richest and most powerful man in the county. Anna and Drew fawn over Ashwin all the time, and I'm forever bombarded with their arguments over who will eventually get to marry him. I personally don't think my stepsisters should be allowed to marry anyone, even if there was someone who would take them.

Now that I know who he is, I can remember where I've seen Ashwin before. Anna and Drew each have his framed portrait in their rooms, which I get to dust every other day.

"Can you not speak?" Ashwin asks.

"I ... I'm sorry," I say, dipping my head, and offering a small curtsey, an action that doesn't appear very ladylike when wearing old hand-me-down trousers with the knees worn through. The result of scrubbing many floors at Roche Manor.

Ashwin chuckles. "Don't do that, you look ridiculous."

"Sorry," I mumble, clasping my hands in front of me, and staring down at them.

"Don't do that, either. I'd like to see your eyes. And stop apologising."

I look up again, heat creeping into my cheeks, sure that my face has turned an embarrassing shade of crimson. I don't have the chance to spend much time with boys, or anyone really. I've never met Ashwin before because Mother home schooled me before she got sick, then I spent my time nursing her. Now, I'm usually too busy with chores and lessons to have any friends, and all my spare time is spent visiting the cemetery. If my stepmother, Lady Roche, had her way, I would never be allowed to leave the grounds of Roche Manor.

"Are you going to tell me your name?" Ashwin asks.

"It's Eleanor." I don't tell him I go by Ella, and that no one calls me by my real name, even though I prefer it.

"You should be careful, Eleanor," Ashwin says. "Using magic can get you into a lot of trouble."

"Why?" I raise my chin in defiance. "I know what I'm doing."

"Who taught you? And where did you get that artefact?"

"My mother." I curl my fingers around my pendant. "And I rightfully own it. Which means I also have the right to use it."

Ashwin narrows his eyes. "Where are you from? I haven't seen you around before."

I hesitate. He has a funny way of going about getting to know someone he has just met. Why is he giving me the third degree? How dare he come up here and demand these answers of me? Although, I don't voice my opinion. It's one thing for someone to be rude to me, but another for me to be rude back.

"I'm not comfortable telling someone I don't know where I live," I finally say.

"Well, you mustn't live near Chethan Manor." He looks me up and down. "In the village, perhaps?"

"And what are you trying to imply? Just because you haven't seen me before, and I'm not dressed fancy like you, doesn't mean I don't have the right to be here."

Ashwin glances at my mother's headstone. "My apologies for your loss, although I don't recognise the name. I admit I've not been to this part of the cemetery before."

I'm glad my mother's memorial doesn't have my father's surname on it. They were never formally married, which is why Lady Roche is so terrible to me. She thinks I'm illegitimate, and that she therefore has more right to Roche Manor than I do.

I stare at Ashwin, not sure how to respond to him. I'm doing my best to remain polite, but he obviously thinks I'm beneath him. Which unfortunately I am, but how dare he think that?

"What exactly are you doing in this part of the cemetery?"

ELLA and ASH

I fold my arms over my chest, and feel self-conscious dressed like a scruffy stable hand. "Do you have a loved one all the way up here?"

"Not exactly." Ashwin looks out over the main part of the cemetery, which spreads into the distance along the hillside. He points towards the road that winds past. "Over there. My brother. He's in the—"

"Section reserved for your family members," I say.

The Chethan family have been in the county for several generations, and are so rich they even have their own section of the cemetery. Like a cemetery within a cemetery. My father and I had to bury my mother in a far off unreserved corner, a good ten-minute walk from the main gates. I prefer it though. It's usually very peaceful up here.

"Yes, there are many Chethans buried down there. Unfortunately, my older brother was lost only months ago. He was nineteen."

"I remember," I say, recalling how horrified my step-sisters were that they had lost a potential husband. "I'm sorry for your loss as well."

Ashwin smiles with a closed mouth. "Thank you. This is the first time I've come to visit since the funeral."

"What brings you all the way up here then?"

"I saw your magic." He studies me, hands back in his pockets. "Why does someone of your standing own such a beautiful magical artefact?"

"*My* standing?" I put my hands on my hips. "What

is wrong with my standing? You don't even know me."

Ashwin looks me up and down again. "Only the highest ranking citizens have access to such things."

I clench my fists, and try to keep an even temper, but this boy is pushing all the wrong buttons. Yes, most of the magical artefacts in the county are owned by the rich, passed down from generation to generation. But there are a few who are lucky enough to have heirlooms, even if they don't have money.

"This pendant was my mother's," I say. "And it was her mother's before that. No one has the right to take it away from me."

"You should be careful with it," Ashwin says. "Some might think you've stolen it."

"Because I'm poor?"

"I apologise if that's what you think I'm implying."

I scoff, because it's very obvious that's what he's trying to say. "You don't know me, and you shouldn't judge me."

"I could say the same to you." Ashwin looks back towards his family plot. "You judged me the moment you found out who I was."

And you are living up to your family's pompous reputation.

I refrain from saying such a thing out loud, and turn away from him towards the willow tree. The leaves sway in the breeze, sending me a subtle message, and I take a moment to check my manners. Mother didn't raise me to be rude, and I won't be, no matter how much I'm goaded.

"Perhaps you should leave now," I say. "It's clear you

don't think much of me."

Am I that transparent? Is it so obvious I'm a servant? I try to keep my clothes clean and mended, and my hair brushed. My hands are always spotless from the endless use of soap. I'm not dirty or offensive looking.

"Now you're putting words in my mouth," Ashwin says.

I turn, and he is so close I almost bump into him. To avoid touching him, I take a step backwards, and the weeping branches of the willow brush my shoulders.

"If you won't leave, then I will."

Ashwin takes a step closer, and I step back again, under the canopy of the willow.

"I apologise if I have made you uncomfortable. I find you rather fascinating."

I frown and purse my lips. "Fascinating? Like observing an experiment?"

Ashwin chuckles. "No. You just ... seem well educated and have good manners, but your clothes—"

"And I suppose you judge everyone by the way they dress?" I snap. "Perhaps you'd get a little further in your relationships if you put aside your prejudices."

"I don't seem to be able to say the right thing, do I?" Ashwin pulls a hand from his pocket and runs his fingers through his dark hair.

"Maybe if you stopped making assumptions, you would get somewhere."

"Okay." He studies me for a moment. "Your pendant. What can it do? My family has many magical artefacts, but I've never seen anything as remarkable as yours."

I clutch the necklace. My stepsisters and stepmother don't know I have a magical artefact, and now that Ashwin does, it worries me. I've kept it hidden from my family because if they did know about it, they would take it away from me. The only people who know it exists are my father, and me. My mother told me the stone holds the tear of an ancient, and very powerful, witch.

"It really isn't that remarkable," I say.

"Are you serious?" Ashwin looks at my hand hiding the pendant. "That's a Paraiba tourmaline. They're quite rare and unique."

I've never heard of a Paraiba tourmaline, but I don't let Ashwin know that. I just thought it was a pretty stone in a filigree setting. I love how it seems to glow on its own, even when I'm not near the willow, or using my magic.

My insides flip at the thought of owning something so rare and precious. All the more reason no one can know about it.

"Please don't tell anyone I have it," I say.

"So it is stolen?"

"No! Of course not. My mother gave it to me." *How many times do I have to tell him?* "She passed it on to me when she died."

Ashwin comes closer, and reaches out to take my hand that's covering the pendant. My brain is screaming at me to move, run away from this boy, but my feet are planted firmly in place. He curls his fingers around mine, and looks into my eyes. I want to look away, but I can't. I'm lost in his stare.

"It's very beautiful," Ashwin says. "What does it do?"

I still can't tear my gaze away from him, and his hand tightens around mine.

"It's connected to the willow ..."

Ashwin raises his eyebrows. "Yes?"

"It ... it's connected to ..." I yank my hand free, and take a few hurried steps back until I hit the tree's trunk. I was about to tell him exactly what my pendant does, even though I don't want to. I frown, and stare at him.

"That's interesting. But what does it do with the tree?" Ashwin looks up at the majestic branches of the willow. Branches that have grown in the time we've been standing here.

A moment ago, while Ashwin was holding my hand, I would have told him everything. I don't know how I was strong enough to pull away. And now, my head feels a little fuzzy, but I'm certain I don't want to tell him anything.

"What did you do to me?" I ask. "You touched me, and ..."

I glance at his left hand. The middle finger is adorned with a black opal set in a wide silver band. The band is plain, but the stone is a glorious kaleidoscope of colours. I know it's his artefact without having to ask, and I definitely won't be letting him touch me again.

Ashwin's gaze connects with mine, and I have the strong urge to flee.

"Tell me about your brother," I say, in an effort to distract him.

He smiles sadly. "There's not much to tell, really. Only that I am not him."

I'm not exactly sure what he means by that, so I don't ask any more questions.

"I should be getting home," I say. "My family will be waiting."

"Where do you live? I can escort you."

I shake my head and step around him, out from under the tree and into the afternoon sunlight. "No, thank you. I can make my own way."

I head off down the hill, the silhouette of Roche Manor looming on the horizon in the distance, and hope that Ashwin won't follow. It takes all my effort not to look back until I reach the main gates of the cemetery. He hasn't moved from where we were standing under the willow tree. To be safe, I take a convoluted route home.

If Ashwin finds out where I live and who I am, there's no way his family will let me keep my pendant.

2

ust swirls into the air as I sweep the kitchen floor.
My stepmother and stepsisters will be down for
breakfast soon, and I need to have everything ready in
time. I slept in this morning, and came over from my
cottage in the woods a little late. I've usually done most
of my kitchen chores by now, but today I haven't even
set the coffee pot on the stove. Lady Roche is even more
horrible if she doesn't get her morning coffee.

My stepsisters tumble into the kitchen, Drew jumping
to snatch something from Anna's hand.

"Show me," Drew demands, jumping again, but failing
to grasp the piece of parchment from her taller sister.

"He handed it to me," Anna replies. "You can look at it when I say you can."

"I'll use my magic on you." Drew puts her hands on her hips. "Then you'll be sorry."

Anna scoffs. "You can't even levitate a pencil."

Drew scowls, but she doesn't retort. Anna is more powerful than her sister, but my magic is more refined than both of theirs put together. I dare not display it in front of them though. Lady Roche has forbidden me to use my magic in the house. I'm too afraid to anyway, because I fear she has put some sort of spell on me, and if I do use magic I don't know what will happen.

Ashwin was right yesterday when he said my magic can get me into trouble. Just not in the way he probably thought.

The girls stop when they reach the table, finally noticing that I'm in the room.

"What are you staring at?" Anna snaps.

I bow my head and don't respond, sweeping the dirt into a corner, and collecting it with the dustpan to put in the bin.

"Come on, I want to see it," Drew whines.

Anna takes her place at the kitchen table, and smooths the parchment out in front of her. I can't see what's written on it from my place at the bench where I'm preparing the coffee pot. I fill the base with water, and the top with beans, before setting it on the stove to brew.

"Oh, he's so handsome." Drew plops down beside her

sister.

"And I'm going to be the one who marries him," Anna says. "You're not good enough for him."

"Yes, I am," Drew huffs.

I glance at the girls as I keep an eye on the coffee pot. The parchment is a pale yellow, and the morning sunlight shines off the gold leaf scroll border. There's a portrait at the top of the page, but I can't quite make out who it is.

"Who are you talking about?" I ask, setting three cups on the bench.

"None of your business," Anna snaps at me again.

I sigh, and turn back to my task. There will never be a day that my stepsisters include me in anything. To them, I'm the servant girl. The stepsister they tell no one about, and it's times like this I wish my father were here so he could see the way they treat me in a house that should be mine. Every time he comes home, my stepmother puts on such a show of how perfect everything is, and how much they love me. She even lets me sleep in the house.

I want to tell Dad it's all a lie, but whenever I try to say something, I get all tongue-tied. It's probably part of the spell I suspect Lady Roche has cast over me. She has my father under a spell, too. He has no idea that she uses her most prized artefact on him. That the tiara she wears forces him to love her. But even if I could tell Father, he wouldn't believe me, and Lady Roche would throw me out altogether. At least this way I have somewhere to sleep and food to eat, and he has a job.

"Both our names are on it," Drew says. "We're *both* invited."

"*You* shouldn't be." Anna looks down her nose at her sister. "You're not in our year at school. You're too young."

Drew scowls. "I'm only a year behind you."

"I suppose it might be all right if you came." Anna smiles down at the invitation. "But I want him all to myself."

"Well, I want him, too."

"He'd never look at you, you're ugly," Anna says.

"I am *not*." Drew smacks her hand on the table.

"What is all this noise?" Lady Roche asks from the doorway.

"Anna called me ugly." Drew crosses her arms and sulks.

"She can't have him," Anna says.

I turn my back on my stepsisters, and busy myself filling the cups with coffee. The sisters are like this every morning, fighting over something or other, but today it's worse than usual.

"What on earth are you talking about?" Lady Roche takes her seat at the head of the table, and I pick up her coffee cup.

"Ashwin Chethan is having a party," Anna says. "I'm going to marry him."

The cup slips from my hand and falls to the floor, shattering and spraying coffee everywhere. All over the front of the cupboards, the table legs, my feet, and Lady

ELLA and ASH

Roche's house dress.

"It's going to be the biggest party of the year," Drew says, as though nothing has happened. "I can't wait to get my gown."

"And we must get the best dresses in town," Anna says. "Oh, Mother. Let me wear the heart-shaped tiara. Ashwin will definitely fall for me then."

Both of them ignore how red Lady Roche's face has turned. It's not surprising though. They never think of anyone but themselves. Not even their mother. And I can't believe Anna asked for the tiara. Lady Roche would never let her touch it. It's under lock and key. I cringe, and wait for the fire to start spitting from Lady Roche's mouth.

"Ella, clean up the mess, you stupid girl. Now I have to change." She stands from her place at the table. "There better be no stains on this dress once it's cleaned."

Lady Roche must be in a good mood this morning. She's usually far harsher on me when I'm clumsy.

"We *can* go to the party," Anna demands. "And you *will* buy us the best dresses."

They are not a questions. They never are with my stepsisters.

"Of course, girls. You may have whatever dress you want. I've already spoken to Lord Chethan. He's most excited about Ashwin turning eighteen. He will be receiving his first artefact. But no, Anna, you are not wearing the tiara. If you want to marry Ashwin, you must win him over the proper way. Not by using magic. Spells don't last forever." She flounces from the room.

I let out a long breath, unable to believe Lady Roche told Anna she can't use magic on Ashwin. She's a hypocrite. And I long for the day her spell on my father, and me, is broken.

But how can Ashwin be receiving his first artefact? He had one on yesterday when I met him in the cemetery. It's usually a big deal when the children of the wealthy come of age. Their parents delight in publicly presenting them with an artefact better than anyone else's.

The better the artefact, the higher the person's standing.

I fetch the dustpan and broom again to clean up the smashed coffee cup. While I'm on my knees, I block out my stepsisters' incessant chatter, and try to think what this means. Ashwin is having a party for his birthday. I wonder what sort of party. A big, fancy, flashy one I bet. I've never been to such an event, but my stepmother and stepsisters have attended a few functions in the county. They are not as wealthy as the Chethans, but they have a good enough standing thanks to my father's money.

"A masquerade ball," Anna says. "It will be so much fun disguising ourselves."

"You *should* cover your face," Drew exclaims. "He won't want to look at something so hideous."

I sigh, and get up from the floor, taking the dustpan to the bin and emptying the contents. Anna and Drew are always either in competition with each other, or putting each other down. There's definitely no love lost between

ELLA AND ASH

them. And the way they treat each other makes me sad. They are both equally beautiful. On the outside at least.

A masquerade ball does sound exciting. I wish I could go. No one would be able to tell who I am if I'm dressed up and wearing a mask. I could enjoy the night free of judgement. If I went, I'd make sure even my stepsisters couldn't recognise me. But there's no chance of me ever getting an invitation. Especially after the way Ashwin treated me at the cemetery yesterday.

I take the girls' coffee cups to the table, glancing down at the invitation. Ashwin is handsome in the portrait, but he's far better looking in real life. If only he were nice, too.

Anna snatches the piece of parchment up, but not before I catch the date ... one week from this coming Saturday.

"There's no way you're going," she snaps, then turns to Drew. "Could you imagine? Ella at a ball in her ripped boy-trousers."

Drew sniggers. "She doesn't even own a dress fit for a ball."

I turn away from them and go to the sink, pumping water to wash the fruit I still need to cut up for their breakfast. There's no point retaliating, it only makes things worse. And technically I do own a dress that's worthy of wearing to a ball. I own a few, only they're in the attic. They belonged to my mother, but after she died and Father went away to work, Lady Roche packed most of Mother's things away and forbade me to go up there. The attic is the only room in the house I'm not required to clean.

Lady Roche comes back into the kitchen, and I hurry to get her a fresh cup of coffee, concentrating on not dropping it this time.

"Ella wants to go to the masquerade ball," Drew says to her mother, a smirk on her face.

I never said that out loud, but this is the sort of thing my stepsisters do to me on a regular basis. It's best for me to keep my head down, do my chores, and respond as little as possible.

Speak only when spoken to. And even then, only if it's necessary.

Lady Roche laughs. "I hope she knows it's invitation only."

Of course I do, I'm not stupid.

I finish serving the girls and Lady Roche breakfast, and tidy the kitchen. Then I set to work on my other chores before I need to get ready for lessons. I press my stepsisters' school dresses, polish their shoes until I can see my face in them, then I make their lunches and pack their bags.

They chatter, and I block it out as I help them both with their hair. Every morning I have to braid and twist and pin their long locks until they are satisfied. One morning Anna made me do her hair thirteen times before she was happy. I usually wear my own golden locks up in a bun. Nothing fancy. Just tucked away to keep it out of my eyes, and off my neck so I don't get too sweaty while I work.

When I've ticked the last box on my list of morning

ELLA AND ASH

chores, I grab some food from the pantry and make my way back to the cottage in the woods via the path from the western side of the grounds of Roche Manor. My stone cottage is tucked away for a reason, so no one really knows I exist. I don't mind living out of the way. It's quiet, and I'm free of Anna and Drew's annoying voices.

As I walk, I pass the stables and wave to Gerald, the stable hand, who is pitching hay from the back of the wagon.

He raises his hand and yells, "Ella, the horses miss you."

"I'll come by soon," I call back.

I love going to the stables, but with chores, and lessons, and visiting the cemetery, I usually only find the time once a week to visit.

When I reach my cottage, I lift the rickety wooden door so it doesn't catch on the uneven ground. The inside of the cottage isn't much—two rooms and a dirt floor—but I love it. It's all I need, and I've done my best to make it my own. I set the apple, bread, and cheese I took from the kitchen on the small table in the corner, and go into my bedroom.

My trousers are dusty and damp from morning chores, so I change into my second pair and put the dirty ones into a bucket to wash later. A small tarnished metal box sits on my side table. I pick it up and open it, taking my pendant out and fastening it around my neck. I dare not wear it in the house. If Lady Roche or my stepsisters see it, they will ask questions. And I don't want to risk losing my artefact.

I sit on the bed and take a moment, closing my eyes and clutching my pendant to calm myself after such a hectic morning. The quilt beneath me is soft with age, and I run my fingertips over the patchwork. It brings back memories of my mother, and how I used to watch her sew.

With a deep breath, I get to my feet and pull a wooden box from under my bed. Inside are the books I need for my lessons. Lady Roche won't allow me to attend the school in the village. She refuses to spend the money. I don't mind though, because I wouldn't really fit in. The only students who attend are from the rich families. The lower classes can't afford such a luxury, and most children get taught at home, like I was before Mother died.

Despite Lady Roche often telling me I'm stupid, I know I'm smart, and every day I study hard so I can do something when I'm older, something other than being a servant. Over the years I've collected Anna and Drew's old books. Drew and I are the same age, with Anna a year older than us, so by the time I get the books I'm already behind. But I do my best to keep up.

I take out a math and a history book, a scrap of parchment, ink and my quill, then go back to the table in the main room. I sit and read, take notes, and pick at the bread and cheese. The apple I will eat later this afternoon.

After a couple of hours, my mind begins to wander to the invitation from Ashwin, and I set my quill down, leaning back in my chair.

ELLA AND ASH

How lovely it would be to go to a masquerade ball. If only I was invited.

Birds chirp outside, and a swallow lands on the windowsill. Seconds later, another one joins it. Their song sounds sweet in my small cottage. I smile and get to my feet, opening the cupboard under the sink to get the small packet of birdseed I keep there.

"Are you hungry today?" I ask.

The birds' song intensifies.

I laugh. "Of course you are."

I sprinkle some seed along the windowsill, and watch the birds peck at it.

"What do *you* think about a masquerade ball?" I ask them. "It would be a fantastic night." I pause, and watch the birds as they hop around, retrieving the seed. "But even if I was invited, there's no way Anna and Drew would allow me to go. And besides, what would I wear?"

One of the birds flits to my shoulder, and gently pecks me on the cheek. It tickles and makes me giggle. The bird grabs the chain around my neck in its little beak and pulls. The stone in the pendant glows a brilliant blue.

"You want me to use my pendant? But I couldn't. Requesting something from the willow for myself has consequences, you know that."

The bird gives the chain around my neck one more tug before returning to the windowsill for more seed. I go back to the table and sit, but I can't do any more study. My mind is whirling with thoughts of beautiful gowns.

There's no doubt the willow tree would be able to give me a dress more beautiful than anything anyone else could sew, but at what cost?

I can't use my pendant for personal gain.

The birds swoop into the cottage, and land on the wooden blanket box set against one wall. It's where I keep my winter blanket, and my meagre wardrobe. The birds dart around, and one leans over the edge, tapping its beak on the latch. There is another blanket box just like it in the attic at Roche Manor. It belonged to my mother, but since Lady Roche forbade me from going anywhere near the top level of the house, I haven't looked at its contents. I'm sure the box holds at least three beautiful gowns.

"You want me to look at my mother's dresses?" I ask the birds.

They break out in song, fluttering into the air and looping around, before landing on the windowsill again. I smile, and the swallows' chatter continues as they fly through the window into the trees outside the cottage.

Maybe tomorrow I'll sneak up to the attic to see what state Mother's dresses are in. My chances of getting an invitation to the ball are pretty much zero, but a girl can dream.

3

Leaves crunch beneath my feet as I walk up the hill towards the willow tree. The autumn days have started to cool in preparation for winter, and I pull my threadbare coat tight around my shoulders.

When I reach the veil of leaves, I run my fingers through them. They sway in the breeze, and the air makes it sound as though the tree is sighing. I part the weeping branches and step through.

A tear rolls down my cheek, and I wait for it to slide off my chin and land on the soil at the base of the tree. The willow grows like it does every time I come here. I shed more tears, and think about the terrible mood Lady

Roche was in this morning. No matter what I did, it wasn't right. It took me all day to do my chores, because she followed me around, making me do everything twice. She didn't leave the house after lunch like she often does, so there was no time for me to sneak up to the attic like I had planned, and no time for lessons.

I couldn't wait to get out of the house.

When my eyes are dry, I go to my mother's grave, kissing my fingertips and pressing them to the top of her headstone. Then I sit on the grass with my legs crossed and face her.

"How are you today?" I ask, like I do every time I visit. "I didn't have a very good morning. Lady Roche and my stepsisters were so horrid. But I have some news." I draw my knees to my chest and hug them.

"Ashwin Chethan is turning eighteen. Did you know the Chethans when you were here? I don't remember meeting many people when I was younger. Father was always away, and I know you liked to keep to yourself. We did have so much fun in the manor though, didn't we?" I pause, and listen to the breeze as it jostles the willow.

"Anyway, I met Ashwin the other day. He was the one who startled me while I was playing with the birds." I pick up a dry leaf and twirl it between my fingers. "He's invited Anna and Drew to a masquerade ball. Of course I can't go. But it's been nice fantasising about dressing up, and wearing a beautiful gown." I stop and smile, glancing at the willow tree that can give me exactly what I want.

ELLA AND ASH

"I would wear one of your dresses, and I would feel like a princess. Even if it was just for one night." I stare at the stone that marks my mother's resting place, wishing she was here so I could tell her all of this in person.

A twig snaps and I jump.

I look up, and Ashwin is standing with the sun behind him, forming a halo around his head.

"I apologise if I startled you," he says. "I hoped I would find you here."

I scramble to my feet, and brush the dirt from the back of my trousers. "Why? What do you want?"

Ashwin raises his eyebrows. "I'm sorry. I'll leave if you like."

I shake my head. "No, I ... It's me who should apologise. I didn't mean to be so rude. I just didn't expect to see you again."

And I hope you didn't hear me talking to my mother about the ball.

"Well, I don't know where you live." Ashwin takes a step forward. "I thought this would be the easiest place to find you.

"I try to come every day," I say.

"You must have been very close with your mother."

I look at my hands, and pick at my fingernails. "She was so sweet, and kind. I miss her. But you don't want to hear my sob story." I glance up. "What brings you here?"

"I wanted to see you again. I fear we may have gotten off on the wrong foot."

I'm unsure how to reply. He wants to see me? Why? We are too different from each other. I will never be good enough for him. Whether I like it or not, I'm a servant girl. And servant girls don't mix well with the rich.

"Maybe," I say. My throat feels thick, and no more words will come out.

I stare out over the cemetery at Roche Manor on the hill behind it, cursing the day my father married that terrible woman. It should be my house. It *is* my house, but Lady Roche renamed it, and she makes sure I get nothing.

Ashwin comes and stands beside me. "Do you know the people who live in Roche Manor?"

"No," I say, a little too quickly.

I wish I didn't know them.

"The house had another name once. I can't remember what it was, though." I catch him glancing at me. "I guess it's not important. I never knew who lived there. Chethan Manor is over the other side of the county. Until my brother died, I didn't have reason to come out here."

Ashwin stares at the house. *My* house. Then continues, "The two girls who live there now, I go to school with them." Ashwin rocks on his heels. "I don't like them much. It's probably a blessing you've not met them. Anna and Drew can be … tedious."

I frown, wondering why he's telling me this. Even though I'm secretly happy he doesn't like my stepsisters, I would never dream of being so up front about it.

"Do you speak this way about everyone?" I ask, facing

him.

Ashwin chuckles, and holds my gaze. "Only the people I don't like."

I offer him a small smile, then turn and walk under the canopy of the willow tree. I sit on the earth and rest my back against the trunk.

The weeping branches part, and Ashwin steps through. "May I sit with you?"

I draw my knees up and hug them, nodding. "You've been here for at least five minutes. Aren't you afraid someone might catch us together?"

Ashwin sits on the ground near me, and crosses his legs. "Why would I care about that?"

"I thought we established I'm not of your standing."

He shrugs. "I'd like to get to know you."

I don't want to talk about myself. My story isn't one I like telling. I glance at Ashwin's hands resting on his knees. "Tell me about your artefact," I say, in an attempt to take the focus off me.

"I asked you first. The other day. About your pendant."

Back to me, then.

"Ah, but you were using your artefact to get me to tell you," I say. "That's cheating."

"How so?" He fiddles with the ring on his finger. "Artefacts are there to be used. What good are they if you can't use them for their intended purpose?"

"Even if that purpose is against any moral standing?"

Ashwin frowns. "I've never thought about it like that."

No. Because families like yours usually get what they want.

He stares at me, but when I don't say anything he continues, "I'm sorry if I invaded your privacy. I should not have tried to force you to tell me something you didn't want to."

"Apology accepted." I smile, and study his face for a moment. He returns a grin, then runs a hand through his hair, blushing. Is he being sincere? Can I trust him? "If I tell you what my pendant does, will you promise never to tell anyone about it?"

"Yes," Ashwin says without hesitating.

"How can I be sure?"

He adjusts his position, uncrossing his legs and leaning on one hand. He holds the other one up so I can see his ring. "You already have an idea of what this does."

"It makes people tell the truth."

"That it does. So … *you* put it on. And then ask me that question again." He slips the ring off his finger, and holds it out to me.

I take it from him and rest it in my palm. The stone is beautiful. The light dances over the rainbow flecks. Apart from my pendant I don't own any other jewellery, and I certainly don't own another artefact. Lady Roche has several, but they're locked away, unless she's out and wants to impress someone.

"Put it on," Ashwin says. "It won't hurt you."

"How do I know you haven't used magic to enchant

it?" I ask. "How do I know it isn't loyal to you?"

Ashwin shrugs. "I've never been very good at simple magic, or casting spells. I'm not much of a wizard. I guess you'll just have to trust me."

The son of the richest family in the county can't do magic? I find that hard to believe. Surely he'd have the most knowledgeable and well-trained tutors at his disposal.

I open my mouth to say so, but Ashwin speaks first.

"I know what you're thinking. I'm rich. I should have the best teachers. But ..." He shrugs again. "Some things can't be taught. Some things ... people aren't good at."

I take a breath, and slip the ring onto my thumb because the band is too big for my fingers. I hold my hand out in front of me and study the rainbow stone. Do I *really* want to tell this boy I hardly know about the one thing that's most precious to me? He said he wants to get to know me. It would be nice to have someone I can be with, and talk to, without them snapping at me or ordering me to do something.

A friend.

Someone I can share my secrets with.

I fiddle with the ring on my thumb. "I ask you anything, and you answer truthfully?"

"Yes." Ashwin is smiling when I look at him. "But you have to be touching me."

He leans forward, and holds out his hand. I hesitate before taking it, but when I do his touch makes my insides flip. His skin is smooth and warm. Ashwin runs his thumb over the back of my hand. I stare into his eyes, and feel a connection I can't explain.

I worry at my bottom lip. "Do you promise not to tell anyone about my pendant, or what it can do?"

"I promise," Ashwin replies.

"Are you in the habit of breaking your promises?" I raise my eyebrows.

"No, of course not."

If Ashwin's artefact does what he says it does, then I should be able to trust his words. But if he is somehow lying to me, and he has cast a spell to make it only work for him, I might regret telling him anything.

I take a deep breath. "My pendant is connected to the tree—"

"You already told me that."

"Please don't interrupt," I scold. "It's connected to the willow, and to my mother. They can give me whatever I ask for."

It's Ashwin's turn to raise his eyebrows. "Anything? You could ask it for a chocolate cake with cream and cherries, right now, and we could sit here and enjoy it together?"

"We could." I press my lips together. "But the magic from my pendant ... I can't use it for personal gain. If I do, it comes with consequences."

"What do you mean consequences?"

"It's different each time, depending on what I ask for."

ELLA AND ASH

Ashwin is quiet for a few moments. He lets go of me and sits with his knees up, leaning back on both hands. "How much of this is true?"

"All of it," I say.

Ashwin glances at my hand. "But you're wearing the ring. How—"

"I don't need to be put under a spell to tell you the truth." I take his artefact from my thumb, and pass it back to him.

He cradles the ring in his palm. "Why does the pendant's magic have consequences?"

I pick up a fallen leaf from the ground in front of me, and twirl it between my fingers. "My mother told me that the only way magic can be good, is if it's used for the right reasons. I think she cast a spell on the pendant when she became ill, and she knew it would be passed on to me. Maybe it's her way of helping me to never lose sight of who I am. But maybe, she also wanted to prevent anyone else from using it in the wrong way. This pendant is very powerful."

"So your mother made sure whoever uses it would quickly learn to only use it for good?"

"I think so." I touch the stone in my pendant with my fingertips.

Ashwin slips his ring on and makes a fist. "I inherited this from my brother after he died. He received it for his eighteenth birthday. It was never supposed to be mine."

"And what artefact will you receive for your upcoming

birthday?" The question is out before I remember I don't have an invitation to the ball, and he hasn't told me about it.

Ashwin regards me for a moment. "You know about my party?"

"Don't look so surprised. You're Ashwin Chethan. Everyone in the county knows about it," I say.

The air grows heavy with anticipation, and the willow tree sighs. I hold my breath, waiting for him to say something.

"My new artefact will be a surprise," he finally says. "The masquerade ball is my parents' idea. I'm not really into all the ... extravagance."

"You should tell them that."

"You obviously haven't met my parents." He looks at the ground.

Sadness overwhelms me, because no, I haven't met his parents. I don't get to meet a lot of people in general. Whenever someone comes to the house, I get hidden away out of sight. I'm not supposed to go into the village, even for supplies. They get delivered. The only places Lady Roche allows me to go on my own are the cemetery, and my cottage.

I get to my feet and stretch, shaking out the numbness that has crept into my legs from sitting on the ground. I need to touch the tree. Establishing a connection with it always lifts my spirits.

Ashwin doesn't take his eyes from me as I move towards

the weeping branches of the willow, and run my fingers along them. They sway back and forth, rustling softly.

"You really love this tree," Ashwin says, breaking our silence.

"I planted it the day we buried my mother." I walk the circumference of the willow canopy, losing sight of Ashwin for a moment as I pass around the trunk. When I come full circle, I say, "I should be getting back. Thank you for your company today, Ashwin."

He gets to his feet. "Please, call me Ash. I feel we know each other enough now to lose the formalities."

"Okay then, Ash," I say. But I still don't want him to know I'm called Ella. I like that I have someone who will call me by my full name.

He makes a little bow. "When can I see you again?"

He wants to see me again!

"I ... I'm not sure. I can't always make it to the cemetery."

"Perhaps I could visit you?"

I twist my fingers together. "I'm quite busy this week. Why don't we just leave it to fate?"

I don't want him to find out I'm a servant girl, and there's no way I could have him come to Roche Manor. My stepsisters would be on him like vultures.

"In that case, are you busy next Saturday, a week from tomorrow?"

My heart pounds, and I don't know how to answer. Next Saturday is the ball. Is Ash going to ask me to the ball?

"No, but I have a feeling you are," I say.

"Eleanor, would you like to come to the ball, and help me celebrate my birthday?"

I open and close my mouth a few times, not exactly sure what to say. I can't say no. That would be rude. But if I say yes, how will I be able to get past my stepsisters? They will surely do something to sabotage my efforts. Perhaps if one of Mother's old gowns is beautiful enough, they will let me go. If I don't look like a servant, maybe Lady Roche will allow me this one night.

"I thought it was invitation only," I finally say.

"Well." Ash puts his hands in his pockets, and rocks on his heels. "Consider this your invitation. I would like it if the prettiest girl in the county could be there."

He thinks I'm the prettiest girl in the county!

Warmth creeps into my cheeks, and I stare at my hands, a smile playing at my lips. When I have the courage to look up again, Ash is staring at me with hopeful eyes.

"Thank you for inviting me," I say. "It would be an honour to attend."

4

I'm on my knees in the large foyer of Roche Manor, scrubbing the slate floor, when Anna and Drew come barrelling down the stairs. Their voices vie to be heard first, each of them getting louder, and louder.

"My dress will be prettier than yours," Anna says as she reaches the bottom step.

"I'm going to get the best dress in the county," Drew fires back.

I sit on my haunches and blow some stray hair from my eyes. It falls across my vision again, so I set the scrubbing brush down, and tuck the lock back into my headscarf. I get to my feet, because my knees ache from kneeling.

"What are you looking at?" Anna snaps.

Lady Roche flounces into the foyer. "You will both look splendid at the ball. As will I. Lord Chethan has asked me to chaperone."

Wonderful.

The front door opens, and Lady Roche's driver, Phillip, bows. "The carriage is ready, my lady." He retreats back outside.

"Come on, girls. We have gowns to purchase." Lady Roche claps her hands, then turns to face me. "I want this place spick and span by the time we return this afternoon. Not one speck of dirt anywhere. Do you understand?"

"Yes, of course." I nod.

Anna giggles. "Have fun cleaning the hearth. I dropped the jar of coffee beans, and they went *everywhere.*"

"And the floor in my room," Drew says. "I may have accidently dropped my tea cup this morning."

"I want those beans back in the jar. Every last one. And you'd better clean them," Lady Roche says, before sweeping out the door.

"You might want to fix that, too." Anna points to my cleaning bucket.

I glance around the spotless foyer. "What do you mean?"

"That." Anna waves her hand, and the water sloshes out of the bucket all over the floor.

Drew laughs, and my spiteful stepsisters follow Lady Roche out to the carriage. I want to slam the door, but

ELLA AND ASH

I hold my temper and close it gently, then turn back to the puddle of soapy water I now have to clean up. I sigh, and retrieve the mop from the cleaning cupboard.

Lady Roche and my stepsisters love to shop, so I should have the manor to myself for most of the day, which means I can go up to the attic and look through my mother's belongings. I mentally list all the chores I need to do first. Going to the attic before I'm done with the house is not an option. If I haven't finished cleaning before Lady Roche gets home, there will be trouble. She often makes me go without dinner, but when she's really mad, she casts a spell to stop me from going to the cemetery. I don't want to risk not being able to see my mother for anything.

I work as quickly as I can, cleaning up the water and finishing the foyer. Then I dust the furniture, and sweep and mop the downstairs rooms, avoiding the kitchen because that's a whole job in itself. Upstairs, I continue to work, clearing away Drew's broken tea cup, and scrubbing the tea stains from the floor. I take a brief moment to admire the portrait of Ash that she keeps on her dresser, wishing I could have a picture of him, too. But both my stepsisters would notice if theirs went missing.

In all the bedrooms, I straighten the beds and fluff the pillows, put away clothes, and make sure everything is neat and tidy. Then I give the bathrooms a once over before heading back downstairs to tackle the kitchen.

The place is a mess.

Pots and pans clutter the sink. Food scraps sit on the table and the floor. And Anna has certainly done a good job of scattering the coffee beans from one end of the room to the other. Most of them sit in the ashes of the fireplace, and I wonder how I will ever get them clean.

I sit on a chair at the table, and cry.

I'm never going to have enough time to go up to the attic.

Skittering sounds come from the fireplace, and three mice appear, foraging around in the ashes. One of them picks up a coffee bean, and turns it over in his little front paws.

"What am I going to do?" I ask the mice. "There's too much mess."

The mice scurry over, and climb the leg of my trousers to sit on my knee. The one holding the coffee bean races to my shoulder and pulls back the ratty collar of my top.

"What are you searching for?" I ask. The mouse looks under the fabric again. "I'm not wearing my pendant. You know I don't like to risk it in the house. And I couldn't use it anyway."

The little creature runs down to my hand, this time tugging on my finger, and pressing the coffee bean into my palm.

"You want me to use magic? Well, I haven't done that for a long time. Lady Roche doesn't allow me."

My hand magic has no consequences, but I'm not sure I want to risk using it. What if Lady Roche finds out? What if she really has spelled me? I look around the

ELLA and ASH

kitchen at the mess, positive my stepsisters do things like this just so I have more work to do. *They* use their magic in the house, why can't I? It will only be a quick wave of my hand, and I really want to get to the attic.

"I suppose I could use magic to tidy up," I say. "Lady Roche isn't here. What she doesn't know won't hurt her … or me."

The mice squeak, and scamper back to the floor where they line up in front of the hearth. I stand, and wave my hand in the air towards them. Soft curling tendrils of light come from my fingers and shroud the three mice, turning them a glittering blue. The critters race around the room, retrieving the fallen coffee beans and putting them back in the jar. I sweep my arm in an arc, and magic falls into every nook and cranny of the kitchen, cleaning the surfaces, washing the dishes, and setting everything right.

In minutes, the job is done.

The mice scamper back to the hearth.

"Thank you," I say. "Now I can go to the attic. I do hope my mother has something in her blanket box I can wear. I still can't believe Ash has invited me to the ball."

The mice squeak their approval, and disappear into the dead fireplace.

I waste no more time, heading to the back corner of the manor where there's a door which leads to the attic. The stairs creak as I climb them to the highest room in the house. It has been a long time since I've been up here, and there is a thick layer of dust on everything.

I close the door behind me and find the chain for the light, pulling it to turn it on. A *click* sounds, and the bulb glows. Almost everything up here belonged to my mother. And now it belongs to me—from the antique dresser with the bevel-edged mirror, to the bookcase full of dusty books, to the dressmaker's mannequin in the corner. Not that I can do anything with it all. My cottage is too small.

The blanket box I want to look through sits against the wall near the mannequin. I go to the window first, flip the latch so I can push it open, then quickly check that Lady Roche's carriage hasn't come home yet. The road in the distance is also clear. I make my way over to the wooden box and press my hand to the lid. The polished timber has become roughened over the years, but I love the imperfect, rustic look.

"Please, Mother. Let there be something in here that will make me beautiful," I whisper.

I flip the latch on the front of the box, and lift the lid.

Inside are three gowns, and my heart races as I take the first one out. The fabric is a beautiful soft pink silk with glass beads stitched to the bodice. They look like glitter. The skirt is layers and layers of ruffles. Another dress is made from a darker pink fabric with little flowers embroidered around the sleeves, neckline, and v-shaped waistline.

I drape the two gowns over the arm of an old couch, then go back to the blanket box to look at the last dress.

ELLA AND ASH

Tiny specks of silver are stitched into a sheer overlay that covers the pale gold silk. I hold the dress against me and twirl. The skirt flares out, and it feels like I'm dancing in stars.

Something in the skirt catches my eye, and I stop. There's a tear in the golden fabric. My heart sinks. I will have to repair it and hope no one notices. Or wear one of the other dresses. I sit on the couch, and set the gold dress aside. When I pull the dark pink one onto my lap, I find a hole in it, too. It's mostly along the waistline seam, but the fabric of the bodice is frayed, and will be hard to mend. My heart sinks a little lower. I glance over at the pale pink dress. *Please let it be perfect.* But the ruffles in its skirt are also torn.

I stand from the couch and go to the open window. The sound of birds singing reaches my ears, and I watch two swallows as they play on a tree branch.

"What am I going to do?" I ask them. I lean on the windowsill, and look out at the sunny day. "Perhaps I could fashion a new dress using these. I have all week to work on it. And I could create a masquerade mask to match." The birds tweet their reply, and hop along the branch. "If anything it would mean my dress would be unique."

I pull the window closed, and go to the blanket box to find something to carry the dresses in. I wish I could take the whole thing with me, but it's far too heavy. At the bottom is an old sheet, so I lay it out on the floor, then gather the gowns and put them carefully on top, pulling the corners up and twisting the sheet together to make it easier to carry.

I make sure the attic looks just as it did before I entered, then go back downstairs. I quickly do a final check that the house is in order, and there is no one outside to see me carrying my sheet full of dresses. Then I leave via the back entrance from the kitchen, and make my way into the woods. Excitement courses through me as I walk. I'm eager to get to my cottage, and begin working on my gown.

Once there, I lay the dresses on the table, and retrieve my small sewing basket from my blanket box. For a few minutes I stand and stare at the beautiful fabrics in front of me, piecing a new dress together in my head. I could start with the beaded bodice from the pale pink dress. It sparkles so beautifully, and it's in perfect order.

Bird song fills the cottage. When I turn, the swallows are sitting on the windowsill. The mouse that lives under the kitchen sink pokes its head out.

"What do you think?" I ask them. "Could I make a new gown from these dresses?"

One of the birds flies over, and perches on the pale pink bodice. Then it moves to the skirt of the dark pink dress, and finally, it takes the overlay of the gold dress gently in its beak.

"That's a perfect combination," I say. "But it will be a lot of work." The mouse clambers up onto the chair. The swallows both perch on the handle of my sewing basket, one of them picking up the end of a thread in its beak. I laugh. "I better get to work then."

The birds and the mouse keep me company as I stitch into the afternoon. Before I know it, it's time to go back to the house to prepare dinner, and I've missed my time to visit the cemetery.

"I'm sorry, Mother," I say, running my finger over the stone of my pendant tucked inside its metal box. "I promise I'll come tomorrow."

I gather my sewing supplies and put them away in the blanket box. Then I carefully fold my gown in progress, wrap it in the sheet for protection, and tuck it out of sight.

When I reach the manor, Lady Roche and my stepsisters are flouncing around the parlour, holding dresses against themselves, and arguing over whose is the best.

"Mine is far more beautiful than yours," Anna snaps at her sister.

"Yours looks like a potato sack next to mine," Drew huffs.

"Your dresses are equally fine," Lady Roche says. "It is mine that is best of all." She smiles, and hugs her dress to her chest.

There is no doubt that all of their dresses are magnificent. And I can't see why they are arguing. Anna's is a deep purple with a gold embroidered bodice. Drew's gown is the same style, with emerald green fabric beneath the golden swirls. And Lady Roche holds her black and gold gown at arm's length in admiration.

"They are all beautiful," I say. "You will look splendid

at the ball."

"Oh, *you're* home," Drew says.

"Who said you could talk?" Anna glares at me. "Stop looking at our dresses."

I stare at my feet, and clasp my hands in front of me, wishing my stepsisters wouldn't be so cruel. I was giving them a compliment.

"Take these gowns and put them in the dressing room," Lady Roche orders me. I look up at her and she narrows her eyes. "Then get us dinner. We're hungry from a long day of shopping."

"Yes, Lady Roche," I reply, taking the dresses from the three of them.

"Don't get them dirty," Anna says.

I avoid making eye contact with any of them and go upstairs. In the dressing room, I drape the dresses over the chaise lounge, then wheel out three mannequins from the large walk-in robe. I carefully put each dress onto a mannequin before lining them up along the wall, positioning Lady Roche's in the middle. I sigh, because the gowns are far more beautiful than my dress could ever be.

It's one thing to have an invitation to the ball, and another to be worthy of attending. What will Ash think when I turn up in something more akin to rags than riches?

5

A few days pass. I keep my head down, do my chores, and work on my dress in my spare time, which is often after everyone has gone to bed.

The days have been long, but today Lady Roche is out, and the sisters are at school, so getting everything done is far easier. I manage to get my chores finished and go to the cemetery early. I miss seeing Ash, and I decide not to stay longer to see if he'll come, because this afternoon I want to go and visit Gerald.

The late autumn sun is warm on my face as I cross the grounds of Roche Manor, heading for the stables.

"Hello," I call when I reach the main doors.

"Ella." Gerald comes out of one of the stalls, a pitchfork in his hand. "It's so nice to see you."

"How have you been this week?" I ask.

Gerald rests on his pitchfork. "Oh, ya know. Same as every week. Smokey has missed ya but."

I smile, and walk along to the last stall. "How has he been? Has his leg healed?" I lean on the half-door and look in. Smokey is up the back, favouring his right front leg.

"It's comin' along, but not quite there yet." Gerald comes to my side. "Them barbs on that fence were brutal."

"Come here, boy," I say, clicking my fingers.

Smokey snorts, then hobbles slowly towards me. He nuzzles my hand, and I stroke his velvety nose.

"Lady Roche isn't back yet?" I ask.

"Nah," Gerald says. "Should be soon but."

It's quiet in the stables without the other two horses, and I feel a little sorry for Smokey not having his friends here to talk to.

I spend an hour or so helping Gerald with mucking out the stalls, and putting in fresh hay. Then we clean what tack is still in the storeroom so there won't be as much for Gerald to do when the carriage returns.

"You got 'nough to do in the house," Gerald says. "You don't have ter help me."

I smile at him as I run a cloth over Smokey's saddle. "I like helping you. You're good company. You don't yell and scream at me."

Gerald's eyes glisten. "Such a kind-hearted gal, ye

are, Ella. Thank ye."

Gerald has been at Roche Manor since before my mother died. He was treated far better back then, and every day I wish things could be different for him here. He likes to keep to himself and just do his work. I completely understand. Working and living at Roche Manor can be lonely if you aren't Lady Roche or one of her daughters.

I think about telling Gerald that Ash has invited me to the masquerade ball, but I keep it to myself. Although I trust Gerald, I don't trust that he won't make an absentminded mistake. He's getting on in years, and sometimes he forgets things. If Lady Roche and my stepsisters find out I am secretly sewing a dress, my chances of going to the ball will be over.

I have thought about asking Lady Roche if I can go to the ball, after my dress is finished. But I think it's best to keep it a secret. I will be able to hide behind my mask for the night. They won't recognise me, and I can make sure I get home before they do. We have a second carriage. I can ask Gerald at the last minute to drive me, and Lady Roche will be none the wiser.

A horse neighs from outside, and Gerald and I go to the doors of the stables. The main carriage is coming along the road, so we open the barn ready to receive it. Phillip nods as he pulls in, but he is a man of very few words. He sets to getting the carriage in order while Gerald and I unharness the horses, and lead them around to the stables.

"Ella," Anna's shrill voice calls from the house. "Ella, come here right now!"

I glance at Gerald and sigh. I had hoped to go to my cottage when I finished helping him, to work on my dress. But it doesn't look like I will have the chance now until after dinner.

"Ya better go an see what's up with her," Gerald says.

"I'll see you soon, okay?"

Gerald nods, smiling.

"Good luck," Phillip says as I pass the open barn doors. "She has herself in quite a knot over something. She was yelling at Lady Roche the minute I pulled up outside."

"Ella!" Anna screams again.

"Thank you for the warning," I reply to Phillip, then I take off across the grounds of Roche Manor. "I'm coming," I call.

Anna stands in the doorway, her hands on her hips. "Where have you been? What have you done to my dress?"

I frown. "I haven't done anything to your dress."

"You better fix it or there will be hell to pay."

Anna turns and storms up the stairs. Lady Roche is in the foyer and gives me a stern look. Drew stands at the top of the staircase, staring at me with a smug smile. I follow Anna, wondering what could possibly have happened.

When I reach the dressing room, Anna is pacing, her hands clenched into fists.

"It's ruined," she says. "You've sabotaged my gown."

ELLA AND ASH

I stop in the doorway, but Drew pushes me from behind and I stumble into the room.

"I honestly don't know what you're talking about. The dresses were perfectly fine while I was in here cleaning this morning." I walk over to the mannequin holding Anna's gown and look over it, trying to spot the problem.

Anna turns on me. "You don't want me to go to the ball. *You* did this. You horrible little wretch."

I open my mouth to say something, but snap it closed. There is no use defending myself again, Anna won't listen. She's too worked up, and obviously believes I've done something to her gown.

"What you've done is really quite nasty," Drew says from the chaise lounge. "You're jealous you can't go, so you did this."

I still don't know what the problem is. And Drew is looking rather smug, laying back on the lounge studying her nails. I suspect she has something to do with this, but I can't openly accuse her of such a thing. Despite the fact that Drew is far more likely to sabotage her sister's dress, both of them would rather blame me.

"Please calm down, Anna, and show me what the problem is," I say.

"*This* is the problem." Anna turns the mannequin, and the back of her dress has a tear in it, right down the back from the waist to the bottom hem.

"Oh," I say, because I'm completely lost for words.

It is indeed a horrible thing to have done to such a

beautiful gown. I know I had nothing to do with it, but I don't repeat what I said before. Anna will not believe me.

"*Oh?*" Anna mimics, hands on her hips as she steps towards me. "You better fix it. Right now!" she yells.

"Of course. I'll fix it." I go to the sewing table and pull out the extension. "You will never be able to tell."

Anna huffs. "Come on, Drew. I can't stand the sight of her."

My stepsisters leave the dressing room, slamming the door behind them. I drop onto the lounge and put my face in my hands.

Why are they so cruel? Not only to me, but to each other?

I take a deep breath to compose myself, then stand again. The dress won't fix itself.

With a heavy heart, I get the sewing machine ready, threading it with purple thread to match Anna's gown, then I lay it onto the table to assess the damage. The tear starts at the waist seam, and runs beside the seam at the back. Whoever did this, and I still suspect Drew, knew that it would be able to be mended as though it were new again.

I set to work, pinning the seam and marking where I will need to sew. A little of the fabric will be lost inside the new stitch line, due to the tear not being exactly where the old seam is. But the skirt is so full, it shouldn't be noticeable.

It seems I was optimistic thinking I could use the sewing machine. There is so much fabric I barely get

ELLA AND ASH

halfway up the skirt before the bulk is too much to handle. I stop the treadle, and secure the thread, then move to the lounge and drape the gown over my knees. I'm going to have to sew the rest by hand, and my fingers are terribly sore from working on my own dress.

The task of making so many small, sturdy stitches is an arduous one, and I work all the way up until dinner time. I prepare the evening meal with throbbing fingers, and an aching back. I keep my eyes down, avoiding any chance of conversation with Lady Roche or my stepsisters, then after dinner I get back to it.

I sew on into the night, and it's well after midnight by the time I finish the last stitch. I place the gown back onto the mannequin, lifting it with tired, heavy arms. Then make sure my work is the best it can possibly be. Surely Anna will not be able to find fault with it.

The house is quiet and I tiptoe downstairs, so exhausted I think about sleeping on the lounge in the parlour. But Lady Roche would be horrified if she found me there in the morning, so I slip out the back door and make my way along the path to my cottage.

The night air is crisp, and the grounds of Roche Manor are peaceful in the early morning hour. I let the moonlight guide my steps, and listen to the night creatures scurrying through the forest. By the time I reach my front door, I have woken up a little and feel refreshed.

I light a candle and take my gown out. After stitching for so long on Anna's dress, I really should rest my fingers, but if I'm going to finish my gown, I need to keep working on it. I sew for half an hour. When I can't control my yawns, I pack up my sewing basket, and fold my dress to put it away.

There are still three days until the ball. I'm sure I can finish it by then.

Tomorrow will be a better day, it has to be.

I pull back the covers and fall onto my bed with barely enough energy to drag the sheet over me again. I close my eyes and snuggle into my pillow, hoping for dreams of beautiful gowns, and dancing in Ashwin Chethan's arms.

6

I walk up the hill towards my mother's grave, fixing my gaze on the willow tree swaying in the breeze, glad that in a few minutes I will be able to sit in the shade of its branches.

Lady Roche and my stepsisters have been especially awful to me since the day Anna accused me of sabotaging her gown. My stepfamily have made me work harder, with longer hours, always finding something else for me to do just when I think I'm done for the day.

Anna and Drew have been constantly reminding me that I wasn't invited to Ashwin's masquerade ball, and only someone who was jealous of them would do such a thing to Anna's dress. A few times I have come close to blurting out that yes, I have a personal invitation from Ashwin himself, but I've managed to bite my tongue. If they find out, my chances of going would be completely ruined.

Because they've been so horrible, I haven't managed to make it to the cemetery since then, so I haven't been able to see Ash. The ball is tomorrow, and I have no idea if he even still wants me to come.

I water the tree with my tears. Then I kneel on the grass at the foot of my mother's grave, and press a kiss to her headstone with my fingers.

"Hi, Mother," I say. "How are you? I've had a tough week, but my dress is coming along nicely. I think I'll have it finished tonight. And it may not be as splendid as Lady Roche's gown, but it's mine, and I love it." I pause, and listen to the breeze blowing through the willow tree. "Wearing it will make me feel like you're there with me. Which makes it even more special." I don't tell her what happened with Anna's dress. I want to put that behind me.

I clutch my pendant and close my eyes, recalling my mother's face, and pretending she is with me now. I feel the essence of the willow tree reach out to me and warm my soul.

"Eleanor," a voice says.

I open my eyes, and Ash is standing a few metres away. I scramble to my feet, a hot blush creeping up my neck and into my cheeks.

"Hi, Ash," I say.

ELLA AND ASH

"I haven't seen you all week. Where have you been?" He has his hands in his pockets, like he often does.

"I just haven't had the time to get here the past few days. It's nice to see you." I smile.

"Are you looking forward to tomorrow night?"

My smile widens into a grin. "Yes, I am. That is, if you still want me to come?"

"Of course." He pulls his hands from his pockets, and in one of them is a folded piece of parchment. "I thought I should do the formal thing and actually give you an invitation. I've been trying to get it to you all week, but I haven't been able to find out where you live." He holds the parchment out to me.

Without offering a reply, I take the invitation from him and unfold it. It's identical to the one my stepsisters received, only my name is penned in a pretty script at the top.

"Thank you," I say. "I'm looking forward to attending."

Ash stuffs his hands back into his pockets, rocking back and forth on his heels. "Are you busy this afternoon?" He asks. His cheeks redden, and he glances at his feet.

A smile plays at my lips. "I don't need to be anywhere in particular."

Ash looks up. "In that case, would you like to spend the afternoon with me? We could go to Chethan Manor and ride the horses."

"It's been a while since I've ridden a horse."

"Then you should have a wonderful time." He laughs. "I

have a carriage waiting at the main gate. Will you join me?"

"I would love to," I reply, excitement filling my stomach with butterflies.

Ash and I walk down the hill together, towards the main part of the cemetery. I follow him as he weaves between the graves, which are far closer here than they are up the back where Mother is. We reach the section where Ash's family members are buried.

"Can you take me to see your brother?" I stop at the gate leading into the Chethans' private cemetery. "I'd like to pay my respects."

Ash nods and opens the gate for me, then I follow him past a few old graves to the centre of his family plot, marked by a round mausoleum with thick columns and an intricate iron gate. Through the cut out sections, I can just make out the edges of a marble tomb. Ash unlatches the gate, and the hinges squeal as he opens it. We step inside, greeted by the cool air in the dimly lit chamber.

"That's my great, great, great … great grandfather in the middle." Ash points to the large marble resting place in the centre. "Some family members are in caskets under the floor." He looks down at a bronze plaque. "Others are in the nooks." He gestures towards the evenly spaced alcoves set into the curved wall. Not all of them are occupied, but each has a space at the foot of the casket for a vase to sit.

I step slowly towards the one that has the freshest flowers, a bouquet of peonies and roses, reaching out to touch the colourful petals lightly with my fingertips. Above the alcove is a plaque that reads, "Torin Chethan, loved beyond measure".

"I brought them today," Ash says. "Mother likes me to bring flowers whenever I visit."

"They're beautiful," I whisper.

"The doctor said he died quickly. He didn't ... suffer."

I stay silent, staring at the flowers, and waiting for Ash to continue. I already know that Torin Chethan died from a terrible accident, falling to his death from a balcony at Chethan Manor. It was all my stepsisters could talk about at the time. But I don't want to interrupt Ash. When my mother passed away, all I wanted was someone to talk to about her. Someone to listen to me.

I had no one.

When Ash doesn't continue, I turn and face him. "You must miss him very much."

Ash smiles sadly. "Yes ... and no. It's a terrible thing to say, but ... I was always second best when he was alive. It's as though I never really existed until he died. Now he's gone, I want nothing more than to be in his shadow again."

"I can't pretend to know how you feel," I say. "But I know how hard it is to lose someone you love."

"Your mother ... how did she die?"

I take a deep breath, and look at my hands, twisting them together. "She was very ill. She died slowly. And I would give anything to have been able to make it less painful for her."

"I'm sorry," Ash says.

I shake my head, and look up. "Don't be. I've made peace with it."

And I have. I've come to accept my lot in life, living for the little moments that make it all worthwhile. Like the way Ash is looking at me now, his head tilted, and a gentle smile on his lips.

"How about that horse ride?" Ash says.

I nod. "Sounds perfect."

I follow Ash back out into the sunshine, and to the carriage waiting at the main gate. Two beautiful white horses stand patiently. The driver nods as we approach.

Travelling in carriages is not something I'm accustomed to lately. Lady Roche would never allow me to use the ones at Roche Manor. If I go anywhere, I walk. Ash opens the small door, and holds my hand as I step up into the carriage.

Ash climbs in beside me, and taps on the roof. "Home, please."

"Yes, sir," the driver says, and we pull onto the road.

I let out a startled cry as one of the carriage wheels hits a ditch.

"Everything okay?" Ash asks.

"Yes. I'm fine. Thank you." I'm not about to admit it's been a while since I've ridden in a carriage, and I've forgotten what it feels like.

Ash reaches over and takes my hand. I let him hold it, but I look out the window, because I don't want him to see how red my cheeks probably are. His touch is warm, and I have to remind myself that his artefact will make me tell him the truth if he asks me anything while he's touching me.

It takes about fifteen minutes to reach the outskirts of the village. The carriage winds through the main street, and I watch people walking about, coming in and out of shops and cafes. Some stop to wave at Ash, and others stare with questioning looks. They're probably wondering who is travelling with the county's richest boy.

I haven't ventured into the village since before my mother died, and there are so many things to see, I don't know what to look at first. I wish I was able to come here more often.

Before I know it, we've passed through and are out the other side, surrounded by rolling green hills, and the countryside that is more familiar to me. Chethan Manor is at the opposite end of the county to Roche Manor and the cemetery. I have not been out this way since I was a little girl.

The carriage rocks as we follow the road. I concentrate on the feeling of Ash's hand in mine. We pass another carriage, then Ash points out the window at a huge house in the distance, nestled between two hills and surrounded by manicured pastures.

"Chethan Manor," I say. "It's beautiful."

"Not as beautiful as you."

I glance at Ash then look to our clasped hands, unsure

how to reply. He gives my hand a gentle squeeze.

"Take us to the stables, please," Ash says to the driver.

"Yes, sir." He turns off the main road and heads up a long drive. It takes another five minutes until we pass the huge front entrance to Chethan Manor, continuing along a private road to a stable big enough to house fifty horses. It's far bigger than the ten-berth stables at Roche Manor.

When the carriage stops, Ash jumps down and holds the door open, offering me his hand. I'm not accustomed to people doing nice things for me, and his gentlemanly actions warm my heart.

"My lady." Ash grips my fingers.

"Thank you," I say, allowing him to help me from the carriage.

Ash leads me into the stables, and the smell of damp hay hits me. A horse neighs. And then another. I smile at the sounds of them talking to each other. It was sad to see Smokey on his own the other day. Animals like company just as much as humans.

Of the many stalls in the stable, about half of them are occupied. At a quick glance, I count around twenty horses. They are all different and all equally magnificent, but a striking grey mare catches my eye. She brays and tosses her head. Her nostrils flare.

I walk up to her slowly with my hand out, and she nuzzles my fingers. Her soft lips tickle my skin, making me giggle. She tosses her head again and neighs, before letting me stroke her nose.

"Hello there," I say.

Ash stands beside me. "This is Mariah. And you're the only person in a long time who has been able to do that."

"What do you mean?" I look at him. "Pat her?"

"Mariah doesn't usually like being touched. It takes great effort to get a halter on her these days. So she mostly hangs out in the stables."

I turn back to the grey mare. "When was she last ridden?"

Ash is silent for a moment. "Before my brother died. She was his horse."

"Oh." I stare into the horse's eyes.

I'm lost for words. There's nothing I can say that will make Ash feel better about Torin's death. I didn't know him. And it's not my place to pretend that I did.

I stroke Mariah's nose again, then run my palm over her cheek and down her neck. She tosses her head and brays, before settling and nudging my shoulder.

"I bet you would love to go out. Can I ride her?" I turn to Ash.

He raises his eyebrows. "If you have a death wish. You said you haven't ridden for a while."

"I'm sure I'll remember how. And she can't be that bad. She's perfectly calm at the moment." I continue to stroke the horse's neck.

"She used to be like this all the time."

"Then what are you worried about?"

"Only that you *just* said it's been a while since your last ride. And Mariah has been quite skittish."

I lean over the stall door, and press my cheek to Mariah's neck. She dips her head, resting her chin on my shoulder.

"But ... she seems to like you," Ash continues. "If you can get a bridle on her with no trouble, I'll saddle her."

"Thank you." I smile.

Ash walks along the central corridor of the stables, and stops a few stalls down. There are ropes and leather straps of all kinds hanging from hooks on the wall. He takes down a bridal. I haven't ridden a horse since before my mother died, but I know enough about the equipment needed. The stables at Roche Manor are one of my favourite places. I really should go and see Gerald more often.

When Ash returns, he holds the bridal up, letting the reins hang to the floor. "This is the bit." He points to the metal part. "You need to get it in her mouth, put this top strap over her ears, and buckle it under her chin."

I've seen Gerald do this a hundred times, and my father a hundred times before that. He used to let me tack the horses when I was younger, but I don't tell Ash. I take the bridle from him, and hold it in both hands.

"Are you ready, girl?" I say to Mariah. The horse flares her nostrils. "I'll take that as a yes." I move slowly towards her, the bit in my left hand, and the top loop of the bridle in my right. When I lift my arms, she tosses her head again. "Easy, girl. I won't hurt you."

ELLA AND ASH

Mariah settles, and I push the bit into her mouth. She bites down on it as I slip the bridle over her ears and fasten the strap.

"You made that look very easy," Ash says.

"All you have to do is talk to them nicely. And I have bridled a horse before."

Ash grins. "I'll grab a saddle. You can go in." He opens the door at the end of the stall. "Back in a second."

Ash walks to where he retrieved the bridle from, and disappears through a doorway. I enter the stall then walk around to Mariah's head to hold her reins, running my hand along her smooth coat—a beautiful mottled grey. Ash returns, lugging an intricately embossed, brown leather saddle.

"She seems to be really comfortable having you here," Ash says. "Just hold her reins while I put this on." I nod, and he heaves the saddle onto Mariah's back. She jostles on her feet, but doesn't otherwise protest. Ash shakes his head. "What is it about you? The last time I did this, she tried to kick me."

"I have a way with animals."

Ever since I was little, I've talked to animals. Birds, mice, horses—I love them all. They listen without judgement. But I can't tell Ash that, he'll think I'm crazy.

"You certainly do." He reaches under Mariah's belly and buckles the saddle, pulling tight on the straps. "You can lead her outside if you like." He holds the stall door open. "I'll saddle Storm, and be with you in a few minutes."

I lead Mariah into the afternoon sunshine to wait for Ash. From the stables I look out over Chethan Manor. The grounds are vast. Far bigger than Roche Manor. The house stands to my right, surrounded by manicured gardens that sprawl from the majestic home.

I try to picture what the ballroom might be like, but I have nothing other than the ballroom at Roche Manor to go by. I have a feeling the ballroom at Chethan would be far grander, and I'm excited that I will be able to see it firsthand tomorrow night.

To my left the grounds spread as far as I can see. Rolling hills, and dipping valleys of green. I'm anxious to get going. To have the wind in my hair as Mariah gallops.

"You'll be kind to me, won't you?" I stroke her neck. "You're such a lovely creature. And I can feel how sad you are. Being outside will be good. For both of us. I haven't done this in a while. I'm trusting you to take care of me."

"I hope she will," Ash says. "She was such a wonderful ride before Torin ..."

I look around Mariah to Ash who is standing with a black stallion.

"Storm is the perfect name for him," I say, to take his mind off his brother. "He's magnificent."

"He's a loyal steed. Would you like help getting on?" Ash points to Mariah.

I glance at the stirrups. Mariah is a decent sized horse, but I should be able to pull myself up. "I'm not sure."

"Hold the reins, and grab the saddle. Then right foot

in the stirrup. Left leg over."

"I remember," I say, giggling.

But I fail my first attempt.

I try again, laughing harder when Mariah takes a couple of steps forward, and I almost fall over. "She is quite tall."

"Let me help." Ash puts his hands on my waist from behind. "Pull on the saddle, then leg up."

The warmth of his touch seeps through my thin cotton top. I glance at him over my shoulder, and his face is close enough I could kiss him. For a moment, I'm frozen, hoping he will do just that.

Kiss me.

Then he's lifting me, and I'm in the saddle, looking down at his handsome face.

"Are you positive you'll be okay?" Ash stares up at me.

I grasp the reins in my left hand and lean forward, rubbing Mariah's neck with my right. "I'm sure."

"Okay, then." Ash mounts Storm. "Let's see if you can keep up."

He jabs Storm in the sides with his heels, and the stallion takes off. Mariah follows without any guidance from me, and I cry out in surprise.

"Look after me, girl." I twist my fingers into Mariah's mane, and press my knees inward.

Within minutes we're at a full gallop, the two horses flying over the hillside. Mariah follows Storm, and I hang on as tight as I can. Mariah and I fall into a rhythm. It feels great to be on a horse again, but then she missteps and I jerk in the saddle. Fear rises into my chest. I don't want to fall off.

Ash and Storm come to a stop up ahead. I pull back on Mariah's reins. She tosses her head, finally coming to a jerky halt a few lengths past Ash. My heart races as I take short breaths, trying to calm myself.

Ash laughs. "Too much?"

"Fast," I say. "They can certainly run."

"How about we walk for a while instead? We can go down to the river."

"Sounds nice."

Ash manoeuvres Storm until the stallion is beside Mariah. They nuzzle each other, and my heart fills with warmth.

Then Storm brays loudly and rears up, his front hooves scrambling in the air. Ash fumbles with the reins, his eyes wide. Mariah shies away. Ash hits the ground. Storm bolts as Ash rolls and gets to his feet.

"What happened?" I ask.

Ash brushes himself off. "I have no idea. But something spooked him."

"Look out," I yell, pointing at the grass. "Snake!"

The tall blades sway a couple of metres from Ash's feet. He stands still, his knees bent and his hands away from his sides, ready to run. The snake rears up and hisses.

Ash will never be able to move fast enough.

"Don't," I say. "If you run, it will strike."

ELLA AND ASH

Mariah neighs, and the snake turns its attention to the horse. She stamps her hoof, and tosses her head so roughly I lose my grip on her reins.

"Pull back," Ash says. "Pull the reins and she'll walk backwards."

I fumble for them, but the snake is moving towards Ash. It rises higher.

Then it strikes.

"No!" I lean forward and stretch out my hand.

My pendant sways, and the stone glows. Blue light streams from my fingertips, forming a barrier between Ash and the snake. The reptile hits it and falls to the grass, slithering away. Ash steps backwards and trips, landing on his back in the grass.

He stares up at me from the ground. "Thank you."

I smile, but it falls away when I look at Storm. The beautiful black stallion is writhing on the ground, frothing at the mouth.

"You can thank me when we save your horse."

Ash follows my line of sight. Then he's up on Mariah's back, sitting behind me, in one smooth motion. He reaches around me and takes the reins. Mariah jolts forward towards Storm.

"Snake bite," I say.

Ash jumps down from Mariah's back, and offers me his hand. I take it and dismount.

"What do we do?" He keeps his distance from Storm's flailing legs.

I don't respond, instead moving to the horse's head, and laying my shaky palm flat on his cheek.

"It's okay, boy," I say. "I'm here. You'll be all right."

I grip my pendant with my free hand, feeling the power of love and compassion course through me. I weep for Storm and his suffering, my tears falling onto his black coat. When they hit his hair, they turn a brilliant blue before seeping into his skin. Moments later, Storm becomes still. He flares his nostrils, and twitches his ears. Then he lifts his head. I step back as the stallion gets to his feet. Storm tosses his head, brays loudly, then goes to Ash and nuzzles his chest.

"Wow," Ash says, stroking Storm's nose. "That was incredible."

"I'm just glad Storm is all right," I say.

Ash stares into my eyes. "*You* are incredible, Eleanor."

My cheeks grow hot. "Race you back to the stables," I say to change the subject. "After you help me back onto Mariah."

Ash chuckles, and this time when he puts his hands on my waist, I want him to hold me forever.

7

After our horse ride, Ash takes me back to the cemetery. I use the excuse that I want to see my mother again before I go home. His eyes plead for me to tell him where I live, but he doesn't ask. I can't let him know. Not yet.

"Thank you for a wonderful afternoon," I say, when I'm out of the carriage.

"See you tomorrow night?"

"Of course." I curtsey in my trousers, and Ash laughs. "Tomorrow I will do that in a gown."

"I can't wait to see you again." He stares down at me.

I turn and walk into the cemetery without looking back. I fear if I do, I will run to him and tell him everything.

I *so* want to tell him who I really am.

I make a promise to myself that I will tell Ash after the ball. I just want to enjoy one perfect night, then I will face the consequences of keeping my secret. Of not telling him Anna and Drew are my stepsisters, and I am their servant.

When I arrive home, I have to make a conscious effort not to smile too much. If I do, Lady Roche and my stepsisters will wonder why I'm so happy. I manage to get through dinner and my nightly chores without my family paying much attention to me. My stepsisters are too caught up in their chatter about the ball.

By the time I make it back to my cottage I'm exhausted, but I stay up until midnight, adding the final touches to my dress, then fall into bed.

When I wake the next morning, I'm smiling before I even get up, because today is the day of the ball. I stretch and look at my gown draped over the back of my chair, taking a moment to admire my work. I have nowhere to hang it, so I get up and make the bed, then lay my dress flat on top so it won't crease. I put the mask next to it. To keep my creation out of sight, I cover the dress with the sheet I used to carry my mother's gowns from the manor. I quickly finish getting ready, glance at the invitation sitting beside my pendant box on the side table, then leave for the manor, making sure the front door is firmly closed.

I'm so excited I'm not sure how I will get through the day.

ELLA AND ASH

When I enter the kitchen via the back door, Anna and Drew are already arguing.

"Ashwin won't be able to take his eyes off me," Anna declares. "There's no way he'll look at you." She glares at Drew.

"Of course he'll be looking at me." Drew stands beside the hearth with her hands on her hips. "I'm far more beautiful than you. And my dress is better."

I keep my head down and go through the motions, preparing breakfast, scrubbing the bench, then cleaning up afterwards. I don't want to get involved in their argument. Both their dresses are beautiful, they are just too pig-headed to realise it.

"What do you think, Ella?" Anna asks. "Whose dress is better?"

I look up from my chores. "It doesn't matter what I think. It only matters what Ashwin thinks. And I'm sure he will agree that both of you are equally pretty."

Anna frowns, and screws up her nose. I smile and go back to work, humming as I whip around the kitchen, tidying up.

"Pretty?" Drew says. "We're not pretty."

No, you're not.

"We're beautiful," Anna replies.

I bite my tongue, like I often do. One day I fear I will just burst, and tell them what I really think: that looks are not everything, and they are the ugliest people I know. That they are selfish, and cruel, and Ashwin would never want to be with either of them. I taste blood, and force a smile, relaxing my clenched jaw.

"Whatever you say, Anna." I wipe my hands on my trousers, and hang the tea towel on the rack.

Drew stares at me, cocking her head to one side. "Why are you so happy this morning? Anna, doesn't Ella seem too chirpy for someone who's not going to the ball?"

I look from one stepsister to the other and back again, keeping the smile on my face as neutral as possible.

"She does look a bit perkier than usual." Anna rises from her seat at the table. "What's going on?"

"Nothing is going on," I say. "Please excuse me, I have the rest of the house to clean."

I make my way towards the door that leads out to the hallway. Lady Roche reaches the bottom of the stairs as I come into the foyer.

"You are not going anywhere today until this place is spotless," she says.

"Good morning, Lady Roche," I reply. "I'll be sure to make everything just the way you like it."

"And you must be here to dress us for this evening."

"Yes, ma'am, I will." I stand with my hands clasped together, waiting for her dismissal.

She stares at me for a moment. "You seem … different this morning. What has happened?"

"Nothing, Lady Roche," I say. "Perhaps I'm excited to see you and my stepsisters all dressed up tonight."

Lady Roche looks down her nose. "Off you go, then." She

ELLA AND ASH

waves her hand at me, then turns towards the kitchen.

I let out a long breath, and set to ticking all the chores I have off my list. I'm done downstairs in time to return to the kitchen and prepare lunch. My stepsisters have been upstairs all morning, and I hum to myself in the quiet kitchen, laying out a spread of cold meats, cheeses, and fruit.

"Why are you humming?" Drew asks from the doorway.

I don't answer, and simply smile at her. I'm not going to let anyone ruin my mood today, because come tonight, I will be dancing at the masquerade ball, celebrating Ash's birthday with him.

Anna barges into the kitchen, shouldering her sister out of the way. "Is lunch ready?"

"Don't push *me*," Drew says.

Anna ignores her, plonking down at the table and helping herself to the food. Drew sits as well, then Lady Roche appears. I wash the dishes while the three of them eat without talking, too busy stuffing their faces. When they've finished their plates, I clear the table, setting aside a small meal for myself.

"I'm going out for the afternoon," Lady Roche announces. "Ella, make sure you are back from the cemetery by four o'clock. We need to be ready for the ball by seven."

"Yes, of course," I say.

"Yes, of course," Anna mimics me.

I make sure not to react, keeping my smile in place. Lady Roche clicks her tongue, but she doesn't scold her daughter for being so rude, then she leaves. If only Anna and Drew knew what Ash really thinks of them. *Tedious*, is what he told me. I would also add mean, spiteful, rude, and arrogant, to the list.

"Oh, you're boring," Anna says to me.

"Let's go and look at our gowns." Drew tugs her sister's hand, and they leave the kitchen.

I finally have the chance to eat, so I sit at the table alone to have my lunch. While I nibble on a piece of cheese, I close my eyes and picture my dress. It has turned out better than I expected, and I especially love the sheer fabric that covers the skirt. I can't wait to dance and twirl tonight, and watch the silver sparkle around me.

I finish eating and tidy up before going upstairs to complete my chores. I change the beds, fluff all the pillows, clean the bathrooms, and do the dusting. I'm almost finished mopping the hallway floor when Anna and Drew come out of the dressing room.

"We're going to have so much fun tonight," Drew says.

"Yes." Anna sticks her nose in the air, then glares at me. "And you're going to be stuck here. All alone."

I continue to work, and attempt to ignore my stepsisters.

"Ella would never get invited to a ball," Anna says, following me up the hall as I mop.

"She wouldn't get invited anywhere." Drew laughs.

"Could you imagine?" Anna laughs, too. "Turning up dressed in rags."

"I don't think she owns anything that doesn't have

ELLA AND ASH

a hole in it."

I hum as I mop. The girls walk on the wet floor, but I won't let their cruelty ruin my mood. They have no idea I'll be there tonight, and they won't recognise me. They're so used to seeing me in my ratty boy-clothes.

"Ashwin would never look at her in a million years," Anna says.

I smile to myself, remembering the way Ashwin looked at me yesterday when he told me I'm incredible.

"Why are you smiling?" Drew says. "You should at least be angry at us."

"You usually get all huffy, and screw your face up." Anna stands in my path, and puts her hands on her hips.

I set the mop in the bucket and grip the handle, looking at her. "Does it upset you that maybe I've decided I'm not going to let you get to me anymore?"

Anna narrows her eyes. "There's something going on. And I'm going to find out what it is. You're never this happy. Come on, Drew."

Anna marches off down the hall towards her room. Drew follows, and I wait until they are out of sight before re-mopping the sections of the floor they walked on.

Once my chores are done, I pack away my cleaning supplies and head downstairs to the kitchen. I grab some bread, meat, cheese, and fruit for dinner later, then make my way to my cottage.

When I get there, I put the food into the meat safe, then pump some water into the sink to wash my face and hands. I change into a clean pair of trousers and my favourite long-sleeved cotton top, before peeking under the sheet and admiring the gown that's spread over the bed. I take the mask I made from scraps from each dress, and put it on, smiling at my reflection in the small mirror on my dresser. I can't wait to dance with Ash at the ball tonight.

I slip the mask back under the sheet, and fluff the skirt of the dress to freshen it up. Ash's invitation is on my side table where I left it. I pick it up and run my finger over the gold leaf. My cheeks ache from smiling so much. I fold the parchment and open my silver box, take my pendant out and slip the invitation inside before closing the lid. I put on my pendant then head outside to walk to the cemetery. I haven't told Mother I finished my gown, and I also want to sit and connect with the willow so I can calm my nerves before tonight.

A breeze whips around me as I walk through the grounds of Roche Manor to the road. I pull my sleeves over my hands then cross my arms against the chill. The walk to the cemetery takes about twenty minutes, and I move briskly, eager to get there. I like the burn I get in my legs from walking fast.

I push the front gate of the cemetery open enough so I can slip through, then make my way up the hill to the willow tree. The breeze is blowing stronger here, and the weeping branches sway.

"How are you?" I ask, sitting at my mother's grave

and reaching out to touch the cool stone. "I finished my dress. It's so beautiful. I wish you could be here to see it." The wind whips my hair around my face, and I take the ribbon out so I can retie it. "Anna and Drew were especially horrid today. But I managed to keep smiling. I'm too excited about tonight."

I go quiet, and listen to the sound of the wind in the willow. I close my eyes, and I let my happiness fill me from head to toe. I press my palms onto the grass at the base of my mother's headstone, feeling the sharpness of the blades against my skin. I don't need to tell my mother anything else. The tree sighs in the breeze, and I know she is as happy as I am.

I get to my feet, walk under the canopy of the willow, and rest my palm against the rough bark of the trunk. Tears well in my eyes and I lean forward, blinking to let each drop of moisture fall onto the earth.

"Eleanor," someone calls.

I move away from the tree and back into the open. Ash is halfway up the hill.

"Ash? What are you doing here?"

He reaches me, a little out of breath. "I was hoping I'd find you here today."

"You should be at home getting ready for tonight. I imagine there is plenty to do."

"Mother is taking care of it." He smiles, and it lights up his face. "I wanted to see you before all the pomp and circumstance. Before you don't … look like you anymore."

I frown. "What do you mean?"

"Well." He shrugs. "I assume you'll be getting dressed up."

I laugh. "Everyone will be dressed up. I can't go in my ripped trousers."

Ash chuckles. "I wouldn't mind if you did."

"Getting dressed up will be fun. I'm looking forward to seeing if you can pick me out of the crowd." I beam at him, and I love how comfortable I feel in this moment with him. "Are you okay after yesterday?" I continue. "How is Storm?"

"He's fine. Thanks to you."

My cheeks heat, and I look at my hands. "It was nothing."

"No, it was amazing. Your magic is beautiful. You're beautiful."

I look up again, staring at Ash, unsure if I should believe the words that just came out of his mouth. I turn away, embarrassed, and retreat to the shade and safety of the willow tree.

"Ella, what's wrong?" Ash parts the branches and follows me.

"You can't mean what you just said." Tears well in my eyes.

"What? That you're beautiful?" he asks. "Of course I mean it."

A tear spills onto my cheek and drops off my chin. It looks like I will water the tree twice today.

"Why are you crying?" Ash steps towards me.

ELLA AND ASH

"No one has told me I'm beautiful," I say. "Not since before my mother was alive."

He takes another step, and another, until we're standing almost toe to toe. Ash reaches out and touches my cheek with his fingertips. Then he runs them down my arm and finds my hand, grasping it and squeezing it gently.

"Well ... I'm telling you. You're beautiful, Eleanor."

I open my mouth to reply, but then Ash leans forward and presses his lips to mine. His kiss only lasts a moment, but it's enough to set my heart thumping against my ribcage.

He pulls away and grins. "I'll see you tonight?"

I nod, unable to speak. Ash lets go of my hand, then takes a step back before turning around. I stand under the protection of the willow's branches, and watch him walk down the hill. Once he is out of sight, I run the entire way back to Roche Manor.

Ash thinks I'm beautiful.

And he kissed me!

I make it home before Lady Roche is expecting me, but I don't have enough time to get to the cottage and back. I unclasp my necklace, slipping my pendant into the front pocket of my trousers.

I stop in the foyer of the manor to collect myself. I can't rush in all happy and smiling. My adopted family doesn't like it when I smile. I find Lady Roche and my stepsisters in the parlour.

"Would you like to start getting ready?" I ask them.

Drew smirks. "That's a wonderful idea."

"Yes," Anna says. "We're *so* excited about tonight."

Lady Roche looks me up and down, then gets to her feet. "Come." She waves her hand and walks towards the stairs.

My stepsisters follow her, glancing at me over their shoulders with devilish expressions. Anna sniggers, and Drew raises her eyebrows, smirking. I follow the three of them upstairs, not sure why they're looking at me the way they are.

I enter the dressing room, and understanding punches me in the gut.

My dress is in the middle of the room, on display on a dressmaker's mannequin. Lady Roche, Anna, and Drew's dresses are lined up behind it.

"We found this in your cottage this afternoon," Anna says.

They were in my cottage?

I blink a few times, trying to stay calm and not let them get to me. Maybe now they have seen my dress, I'll be able to go to the ball and not hide it from them.

"Were you planning to go to the ball?" Drew asks.

I look at my stepsister, unsure what to say. Obviously my answer is yes, but I can't seem to get the single word out of my mouth.

"Well?" Lady Roche stands with her hands on her hips. "Were you?"

"What makes *you* think you could go to the ball?"

Anna spits.

"You weren't even invited." Drew's voice rises a few octaves, piercing my eardrums.

"But ... I—"

"But nothing. You are *not* going," Lady Roche says. "Using magic in the house when I have forbidden it is one thing. But going behind my back with something like this. Going up to the attic ... I will not tolerate it."

The attic! She knows I've been in there.

I take a deep breath. "I'm sorry I used magic. But it's just a dance. No one will know who I am with a mask on."

"My word is final."

"Besides, Ashwin would never invite you," Drew says.

"And you can't go if you don't have something to wear." Anna grabs the shoulder of my dress and pulls, ripping the sleeve away from the bodice.

Drew joins her, and all I can do is watch as my stepsisters tear my gown to shreds. They rip off the other sleeve, and yank the overlay away from the skirt, tearing huge holes in it. All my hard work is destroyed in a matter of minutes.

Lady Roche stands tall, a smile on her lips. "Consider this your punishment for disobeying me."

Anger boils inside me, but I force it down. I won't let them get the better of me. I don't want to let them affect me so badly, but this time it's too much. As hard as I try to remain calm, my heart hurts at what they have done. Tears sting my eyes, and I clench my fists.

"You are horrible people," I yell, giving in to my rage.

"Evil, terrible, horrible, nasty, people. You can dress yourselves for the ball."

I turn and run.

Down the stairs, out the front door, and into the grounds of Roche Manor. Tears blur my vision as I stumble across the lawn towards the road. I need to get away from them. How can they be so cruel?

How did they even know I had a dress? Because I went to the attic?

I dig my pendant out of my pocket and put it on, touching the stone with my fingertips.

Maybe using magic has something to do with it. But I didn't use my pendant. All I did was clean the house faster with a flick of my wrist ... so I could go to the attic. Does that count? Did Lady Roche find out because I broke a charm she had set for me?

Have I brought this upon myself?

My feet jar as they pound the road, and I keep running towards the only place where I might find an answer.

I run to the willow tree.

8

The cemetery gate squeals when I push it open. My eyes are blurry from crying, and I stumble as I race up the centre aisle. I fall. Gravel digs into my knees through the holes in my trousers. The pain is sharp.

"Why?" I ask the silent graves. "What did I do to deserve such cruelty?"

There is no answer. Only the sound of the wind as it swirls leaves from the ground. I stay kneeling, and put my face in my hands, sobbing.

Since my mother died, I have taken so much nastiness from my stepmother and stepsisters. But I have always picked myself up again and kept going, no matter what cruel thing they did to me. This time ... I'm not sure if I can get up; even to walk to the willow tree.

They have broken me.

When my knees are numb, and the tears have slowed, I take my hands from my face and stare at the ground in front of me. The gravel is barren. Hard rocks with sharp edges. I long to feel the softness of the grass at my mother's grave beneath my fingertips. I struggle to my feet, and brush the dirt and small pieces of rock from my knees.

I feel as though I can't go on, but I must.

Eleanor. My name floats like a murmur on the breeze.

I look up, my gaze darting around the cemetery. "Who said that?"

Eleanor, my dear. The voice is a whispering sigh, its melodic tune undulating with the swirling wind.

"Mother?" I fix my stare on the willow tree. Its weeping branches sway in the dim light of dusk.

But the voice does not speak again.

I walk briskly towards my safe haven. Towards my mother, and the answers I seek. If only my magic was strong enough to bring her back. If only she hadn't died in the first place, I would not be here, crying from a broken spirit and a broken heart.

The climb up the hill to the willow tree seems harder and longer than it ever has. My shoulders are weighted with sadness, and by the time I reach my mother's grave, my eyes have filled with fresh tears.

ELLA and ASH

I fall onto the ground in front of the headstone, leaning on the rough rock and resting my forehead on my arms. My tears roll off my chin, making dark splotches on the stone.

Eleanor, the voice says again, but when I lift my head to look around, there is no one in sight.

Eleanor, look within, and you will find peace.

"Mother?" I ask. "Is that you?"

A bird chirps, then another, and another. Three swallows land on the ground beside me. One hops onto my knee, then off again, and the three of them take flight, disappear-ing into the weeping branches of the willow.

I look to the tree. Its leaves move gently, and it is then that I realise the voice is one only I can hear. It's the voice of my mother's spirit, speaking to me through the birds and the tree. It is the essence of my magic. I get to my feet and walk under the canopy, letting the tree's leaves shroud me. It sighs when I place my hand on the trunk.

Since my stepsisters destroyed my dress, I have been blinded by my sadness and tears. Now, I stand before the tree and let my last tear fall. It hits the dirt at my feet, soaking into the ground. Blue light rises to the surface, as though it has come from deep within the earth, and seeps up the tree. My pendant glows, and the light stretches to every branch and leaf of the willow, making them grow. The magic wraps its glow around my hand, and reaches out to warm my heart.

You do not need a dress to make you beautiful, the tree whispers, and I feel the words in my soul.

"But I cannot go to the ball in my ripped and stained clothing," I say. "They would never let me in. I would be laughed at, and turned away."

There is no response, and I stand in the glow of the willow, knowing it can give me exactly what I want. But what I want isn't necessarily what I need. Suddenly, the magic from my pendant feels more like a curse than a gift.

What is most important to you? the willow asks.

I concentrate on the rough bark beneath my fingers, searching for an answer that will be true to myself, and not something I think the essence of my mother wants to hear.

"Love. Kindness. But above all, courage," I say. "To get through this."

The tree's branches sway and the birds chirp above.

It was not the consequences of your actions that led your stepsisters to be cruel. It was their selfish hearts. They are responsible for what they do to you. But you are responsible for how you react. If you can forgive them, then you can go to the ball. For it is your love, kindness, and courage, that makes you beautiful.

"It has never been a question of *if* I can forgive them," I say. "I forgive them every day for the things they do to me. My dilemma now, is that I am unable to fix my dress in time to get to Ashwin's party. And I cannot ask you for what I desire, because it is for myself and not another."

Eleanor, you have always been so selfless. You shall go to the ball, and you shall be the most beautiful girl there.

ELLA AND ASH

Wind howls through the branches of the willow. They sway frantically, and the blue light of my magic moves in rhythm with the swirling breeze. Within seconds I am shrouded in light that surrounds me like a hurricane. My hair whips around my face, and I try to calm the movement, but the willow has taken over. I close my eyes, and lean into the magic that is both mine and my mother's.

My skin grows warm, and the sensation seeps into my body, filling me from head to toe. I raise my arms over my head, and fall into the swirl of the wind. Then everything is still. I strain my ears, listening for the sound of my mother's spirit. For the hint of a breath in the willow's branches. But all is quiet.

I open my eyes, and I'm surrounded by a sea of flowing blue silk. I'm wearing the most beautiful dress I have ever laid eyes on. The bodice is fitted to me perfectly, with ruching over the bust. The full skirt shimmers under the light of the just-risen moon. I run my hands over the smooth fabric.

My shoulders are bare. My hair has been pulled away from my face, and left to trail in soft curls down my back. I lift my hands to the mask on my face, running my fingertips over the beading and lace, then I grasp the full skirt of the gown and lift it so I can see my feet. They are encased in delicate slippers, made from glass that sparkles as though there are stars trapped inside them.

The stone in my pendant glows blue, shimmering like my dress.

"Oh ..." I try to speak, but I'm lost for words.

This time, when my eyes fill with tears, they are because of joy and not sadness.

"What price must I pay for this?" I finally manage to ask.

No price, whispers the willow. *But as this day ends and a new one begins, your magic shall also renew.*

I repeat the words in my head. *As this day ends ...* Midnight?

"I have until midnight? But how am I to get to the ball? Chethan Manor is on the other side of the county. It will take me hours to walk there."

The tree does not answer, but one of the swallows flutters to the ground. In its beak it holds a seed. The bird drops it on the dirt, and the seed sends a ripple through the blue magic that surrounds me. A vine sprouts from the ground, snaking off through the cemetery towards the front gate. It grows, and grows, dusted in blue light, until it reaches the road in the distance.

Go, the willow whispers.

I hitch my gown and race off down the hill, trailing the fingers of my free hand along the vine as I run. I'm not sure what to expect when I reach the end. The main gate sits ajar, and I leave the cemetery then come to a stop in front of a glittering silver carriage.

Led by two black horses, the carriage shimmers like starlight. The driver peers down at me and smiles, but he does not speak. A swallow perches on his shoulder, then I see the other two birds, one each sitting between the horses' ears.

I take a step towards the carriage, and the door opens. Inside, the seats are covered with plush red velvet. I set my foot on the step, grasp a small handle near the door, and pull myself up, sitting and tucking my gown around me before closing the door.

The driver flicks the reins and the horses set off, pulling us towards Chethan Manor and Ashwin's masquerade ball. The wheels of the carriage bump over the cobblestones of the main street in the village. When we reach the other side, I grip the top of the door and stare out the open window, fixing my gaze on the lights of Chethan Manor in the distance. I'm eager to arrive and find Ash.

Will he recognise me?

Finally, the enchanted carriage pulls up outside the grand steps of the manor. The driver jumps down from his post, the swallow still sitting on his shoulder, and helps me out.

"Thank you," I say.

He nods, then takes up his driving position and moves off. I flex my fingers to stop them shaking, and look up the stairs to the entrance. Chethan Manor has an exquisite clock set into the face of the building. The hour hand moves closer to eight pm.

I'm almost an hour late, and the party is in full swing. Those who are on the balcony above stare down at me. I keep my head high, lift my skirt, and set a foot on the first step, finding comfort in the fact that no one here knows who I am. I hope my stepmother and stepsisters won't recognise me.

When I reach the top of the stairs, people step aside to let me pass. They stare, faces hidden behind all kinds of masks, but their eyes ask the same question. *Who is she?* Or maybe *I* am simply imagining them saying that, because in this moment I'm unsure if I even know myself.

Stepping into the ballroom is like stepping into a fairy tale. I have to remind myself not to let my mouth drop open. Golden lights drape from the ceiling in delicate strands, leading from the walls to the centre where a glittering crystal chandelier hangs. Recessed arches line the walls, some of them house marble sculptures. A small orchestra plays from a stage at the head of the large room, but perhaps the most magnificent sight is the explosion of colour on the dance floor.

People move this way and that, floating in time to the music. Dresses of every style and colour twirl and flick as the dancers move around the room. I take a few more steps, and a butler greets me, holding a tray of glasses filled with a bubbly liquid.

He bows. "Welcome, my lady. Would you like a drink?"

I curtsey. "No, thank you. I'm fine for now."

He bows again and moves away, on to the next patron. I glance around the room, and spot my stepsisters near the buffet table, taking a drink from another butler's tray. Anna stares at me, then elbows Drew and points. I move in the opposite direction around the room to put some distance between us. I don't want to have to deal with them this early in the night. I'd like to at least find Ash first.

My guess is he will be dancing with some lucky girl. He is the birthday boy after all. As I walk, I search the moving bodies, looking for his mass of dark hair. A couple dances past me, and the boy's gaze connects with mine, but it isn't Ash. The girl puts a hand on his cheek and turns his face back to her. I keep moving towards the stage, standing on my tiptoes to see over the heads.

Then I see him in the middle of the dancing crowd. I immediately know it's Ash. He is wearing a simple mask that covers only his eyes, leaving him completely recognis-able. His lips are curled into a genuine smile. The girl he is dancing with glances in my direction, and Ash follows her line of sight. They spin, and he whips his head around to look at me again as his partner twirls. Then he leads her to the edge of the room, whispers in her ear and passes her to another dancing partner.

When Ash reaches me, he stops a metre away and bows. My arms tremble as I lift my skirt and curtsey in return, unable to contain my happiness any longer. A thrill runs through me just from the way Ash's eyes have lit up.

"Good evening," he says, grinning. "What brings you here tonight?"

"I hear it's someone's birthday." I smile, too.

Ash steps towards me until he can whisper in my ear.

"I noticed your pendant from across the room. You are … stunning."

He isn't touching me, but electricity jumps between us, sparking on my bare skin. I want him to kiss me again, like he did this afternoon, only longer this time. My breath comes in short bursts, then Ash steps back.

"Would you like to dance?" He holds out his hand.

I don't reply, because I can't speak, but I slip my hand into his, and let him lead me onto the dance floor. Ash grips my right hand with his left, and rests the other on my waist. He holds me with his gaze, so intent that even if I wanted to look away, I wouldn't be able to. He moves us around the dance floor, and while I'm staring into his eyes, everything else drops away. We float together, oblivious to everyone and everything around us.

Ash and I dance and dance, song after song, and my feet never feel tired. Other girls try to get his attention, but we are lost in each other. Lost in time and space. It's not until the music stops, and our dancing ends, that I realise everyone else in the room is staring at us.

All eyes are on me, and I have the sudden urge to run.

9

A few seconds seem like a hundred years. I want to shrink away into nothing so all these people will stop staring. I catch the glares from my stepsisters, glad that there are several people between me and them.

Ash bows and kisses the back of my hand. "Thank you for the dance."

I smile at Ash and curtsey, but I notice more looks, and whispers behind hands, from the other girls. To stop myself from trembling, I keep my eyes on him.

Ash leans in and says quietly, "I think every girl in this room wants to be you."

I grip his hand. Right now I'm not sure *I* want to be me.

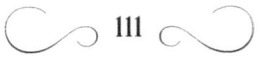

"Can we get some air?" I ask.

But the orchestra pipes up with a loud intro, and Ash's parents walk onto the stage.

Ash squeezes my hand gently. "Can you survive another ten minutes?"

I lean closer to him. "Your artefact?"

He nods, and I face the stage along with the rest of the party-goers.

"Welcome," Lord Chethan says, his wife smiling at his side. "Thank you for coming to help us celebrate a very special occasion. Ashwin's eighteenth birthday, and the presentation of his artefact."

Lord Chethan holds his hand out, pointing towards his son in the crowd, and the room erupts with thunderous applause. I join in, clapping my hands, and smiling at the boy beside me.

"I have to go up there," he whispers. "Will you be okay?"

I nod, because I can't keep him by my side, even though I want to. I'm terrified of every person in this room. When Ash leaves he takes his warmth with him, and I shiver. But I hold my smile in place, and keep my head raised. These people don't know who I am. I just hope I look confident to them, and not scared out of my mind.

The crowd parts for Ash to walk through. He joins his mother and father, standing between them but a couple of steps back. They must have rehearsed this ceremony to prepare for Ash's big night.

A servant walks onto the stage, holding a plush pillow

in both hands. I stand on tiptoe to try to see what is on it, but it's too far away. When he reaches Lady Chethan, the servant bows and holds the small cushion out to her. Ash's mother picks it up and turns to her husband. He takes the artefact off the pillow and holds it in his palm.

"In celebration of Ashwin's eighteenth birthday," Lord Chethan says, "I present to him the Bain pocket watch." He holds it up by the chain, and a brass clock hangs from the end.

A collective gasp circles the room. Even Ash's eyes widen. He must not have been told he was receiving one of the most powerful artefacts in existence. An artefact that no one has seen in a very long time. Even I have heard of the Bain pocket watch, and know what it can do.

It can stop time.

"We entrust you with the protection of this artefact," Lady Chethan says.

Lord Chethan holds out the chain, and Ash steps forward so his father can place the antique watch around his neck. When Ash straightens, light glints from the glass covering the face of the clock. The ballroom falls into an awestruck lull, then applause erupts again, even more ferocious than when Ash was called to the stage. He steps forward, smiling wider than I've ever seen him smile before.

Once the noise dies down, Lady Chethan says, "Please enjoy the rest of the evening."

Ash comes down from the stage, and the orchestra

starts playing again. People take to the dance floor, while others touch Ash as he passes them. He does not stop to talk to anyone until he reaches me.

"Do you still want some air?" he asks.

I nod. He gently takes my hand, leading me towards the exit. We weave through the bodies and then go out to the balcony. When the fresh air hits my face it's a welcome relief.

I lean on the balcony wall and stare out over the grounds of Chethan Manor. The glow from the lights of the main house spread far enough for me to see the beautiful gardens below. The clock above us chimes and I panic for a heartbeat, until I turn to read the time. Eleven pm. I still have an hour before I have to leave.

It's not enough time.

Several girls hover at the balcony doors. Two of them come outside and stand close enough to hear our conversation. I search the faces from the corner of my eye and relax a little when I can't find my stepsisters. I want these girls to go away though, so I can have Ash to myself.

I glance at Ash's new artefact, wishing I could ask him to stop time for us, so we can be here together without the whispers and the stares. But I won't. The Bain pocket watch not only comes with great responsibility, it comes with conditions.

I remember reading about it in one of Anna's old school books. Whoever uses it to stop time, will also lose time. Everything around you may seem like time has stopped, but the clock keeps ticking, and for every minute the hands turn, the user will age that time three-fold.

I reach out and touch the face of the clock resting against Ash's shirt. "This certainly makes your family the richest in the county."

"I don't care about any of that." Ash puts his hand over mine, and presses my palm to his chest. The watch is cool against my skin. "There are other ways to be rich."

I step closer to Ash. So close I could kiss him if I was brave enough.

"You might think differently if you knew who I really am." I stare into his eyes.

"I know who you are, Eleanor."

I stiffen. How could he possibly know? Has someone recognised me? Have I been found out? Is it obvious that I'm a servant girl who doesn't belong here, pretending to be someone she's not?

Is he about to ask me a question I don't want to answer while he's holding my hand and wearing his truth ring?

I shake my head. "You don't understand."

"I don't have to," Ash says. "I don't care where you live, or where you came from. I could've asked you all those questions by now, and you would've told me." He looks down at his ring, the opal shining like a rainbow on his hand that covers mine. "I only care that you are here now. With me." He looks into my eyes again, and I see the truth in them.

My breath catches in my chest, and I don't know how

to respond. There is nothing I can say that will explain how I feel in this moment. A moment where I wish there was no one else around us. I close my eyes, and pretend that I am here with only Ash. I concentrate on the touch of his hand and the tickle of his breath on my cheek. My heart races as I sense him move closer to me still, then comes the soft touch of his lips on mine.

When Ash pulls away, I can't keep the smile from my lips. I want him to kiss me again, but we have a large audience. Instead, I turn my back to the crowd and lean on the balcony wall, gazing out over the gardens.

Ash puts his arm around me. "Thank you for coming tonight."

"Thank *you* for inviting me." I lean into him. "Everything is … perfect."

We talk for a while, and I lose track of time, until a shrill voice interrupts.

"There you are!"

Anna.

Ash pulls away from me and turns to face my stepsister. Anna throws me a death glare, then smiles sweetly at Ash. Seconds later, Drew is at her side. Both girls are beautiful in their gowns and matching masks adorned with crystals and sequins. It's a shame they aren't also beautiful on the inside.

"Hello, Anna. Drew," Ash says. "Are you having a nice night?"

Anna runs her hand up Ash's arm, despite the fact

he is standing so close to me.

"It has been wonderful," Anna croons. "It would be even better if I could have a dance."

"I'm busy right now. Perhaps later." He turns back to me and gives my hand a gentle squeeze.

"Maybe you can introduce us to your friend," Drew says.

My heart races. *Oh no.* If Ash says my name they're going to know it's me. Will my mask be enough to fool them?

"This is Eleanor," Ash says. "And we were talking. If you don't mind."

"Eleanor." Anna raises her eyebrows and looks me up and down, ignoring Ash's blatant suggestion that she should go away. "We have a servant girl with that name. But we call her Ella. Eleanor is such an ugly name."

I hold my breath.

Ash frowns. "It's a very beautiful name in my opinion."

"Oh, well, the Eleanor we know is a wretch," Drew says.

"Yes, she wanted to come tonight," Anna adds. "But we made sure she couldn't."

I can't believe how rude my stepsisters are.

"You shouldn't talk so badly about people when they are not here to defend themselves." I take my hand from Ash's and face my stepsisters. "And jealousy doesn't make you look very pretty."

Anna's mouth drops open. Then she narrows her eyes at me. "Do you know who I am? Obviously not. How dare you speak to me that way?"

I snap my mouth shut in an effort to stop myself from

saying something else I will regret later. But I really want my stepsisters to go away, because I'm running out of time with Ash. Anna takes a step towards me, and I try to move out of the way, but there's no room. My back bumps into the railing of the balcony. The stone edge presses into my skin.

"I think you should back off, Anna," Ash says. "Eleanor is right. Jealousy doesn't look good on anyone."

"What is happening out here?" Lady Roche's voice comes from behind her daughters.

The balcony is now quite crowded, and I want to get away. To go downstairs and run into the open fields so I can breathe properly. But there are too many people between me and the doors.

The clock above us chimes and I glance up as the hour hand ticks over to midnight.

I'm out of time.

Ding ... ding ... ding.

I look over my shoulder to the grounds below. My carriage is waiting at the entrance.

"This girl is being rude to us," Drew says when she sees her mother. "She told Anna she isn't pretty."

I did no such thing, but Lady Roche will believe whatever her daughters say. As she always does. In her eyes, the two girls can do no wrong.

The clock chimes again, and again, and again.

"And who is this girl?" Lady Roche steps forward.

"She is my guest," Ash replies. "And if your daughters

don't check their manners, I will have to ask them to leave."

Ding … ding … ding … ding … ding.

Anna comes closer again, and I lean back with nowhere to go.

"I want to know who you are." Her hand darts out and grabs my mask, pulling it from my face. I stumble forward.

The clock chimes for the twelfth time.

I raise my hands and cry out. Magic shoots from my fingers in a subconscious reaction, and Anna staggers backwards. Ash grabs me and steadies me.

The pendant around my neck glows a brilliant blue. Light flows out of it, down and over my dress, shrouding me in magic that drips from me, slowly revealing my stained top and ripped trousers. I glance over my shoulder, and one of the horses pulling my carriage dissolves. The swallow flutters away. The carriage disintegrates into blue light. The driver falls to the ground, then also disappears before he can get to his feet.

"Ella!" Drew cries. "No, it can't be *you*."

"What is all the yelling out here?" Lord Chethan appears through a break in the crowd. "What is going on?"

"What are you doing here, girl?" Lady Roche asks, ignoring Lord Chethan's questions. "And where did you get that artefact?" She lunges towards me.

"No!" Ash cries.

Everything stops.

Lady Roche is still, with her arm outstretched. I look

down at myself. My dress is gone, but my feet are still encased in the glass slippers. Anna and Drew's faces are frozen in ugly snarls. Everyone else around us stands like statues. I survey the scene in disbelief. Then I look to Ash.

He has the Bain pocket watch open on his palm. The second hand ticks around the face, counting the time it will age him. The time it's taking from him.

I shake my head. "No. Ash. No. Turn it off. Turn it off!"

He doesn't reply. He just smiles and lets the watch fall to his chest, the case still open. Then Ash pulls me to him, and crushes his lips to mine. I fall into him, letting him sweep me away on a wave of longing and passion.

When he pulls back, he stares into my eyes. "I meant what I said. Your name is beautiful. Ella is lovely, too."

I shake my head again, and tears spill onto my cheeks. "Please turn it off. Don't waste time for me."

"You are worth every second."

Despite his kind words, I break away from him. I have to get out of here. The longer I stay, the more time he will lose. I can't let him make this sacrifice for me. I'm just a servant girl. I'm not worth it.

"I have to go," I say.

I run. Through the frozen people and into the ballroom. Out the main entrance and down the steps. I trip, and one of my glass slippers comes off my foot.

"Eleanor, wait," Ash calls, but I take the other shoe off and keep running, through the grounds of Chethan Manor, until I reach the road. Only then do I stop and look back at the lights glowing from the house. At the silhouette of Ash standing on the steps.

A horse neighs in the darkness.

Ash bends to pick something up.

I clutch the slipper to my chest, the last remnant of my magical night, and cry for everything I have lost.

10

I should have been more careful. I should have kept track of time, and left the ball earlier. Before I could get myself into so much trouble. I should never have talked to my stepsisters the way I did. Then Anna would never have ripped the mask from my face, and I would not have thrown her off with my magic.

Now, Lady Roche knows about my pendant, and there is no way she will let me keep it. She will want it for herself. She already thinks everything of mine is hers.

I stumble along the road in the dark, one hand clutching my glass slipper and the other my pendant. The ground digs into the soles of my bare feet. I need to hide my pendant somewhere that it can't be found. My cottage is out of the question, especially now I know my stepsisters have been in there snooping around. Besides, the floor is dirt, so I have no boards to lift.

There are no other places where it would be safe enough, and I need to put it somewhere Lady Roche will never go. The willow will protect it. Lady Roche would never go to visit my mother at the cemetery.

The village is quiet as I pass through, and when I come out the other side, exhaustion threatens to take me. The cemetery seems so far away, but I push on. Finally, I reach the gate with no idea what the hour is. It must be very late. It feels as though I have been walking forever.

I have to stop twice and rest my feet on the way up the hill to my mother's grave. By the time I get there, weariness has seeped into my bones. I fall on my knees in front of her headstone, clutching the glass slipper tightly, and weep.

"I've had such a terrible night. The ball ended in disaster. I don't know what to do," I tell her. "I'm afraid to go home. Lady Roche will be furious. She will demand my pendant."

There is no answer other than the willow's leaves rustling in the light breeze. I get to my feet and go to the trunk of the tree, placing my palm against it and closing my eyes. *Will you keep it safe?* I ask in my mind. I open my eyes, and my tears fall onto the dirt below. They seep into the ground, glowing blue and pulsing in time with my pendant.

Light comes to the surface and swirls into the shape of a swallow. The slipper in my hand also glows. The little bird loops around me, leaving a trail of magic, before it flies up into the tree and perches on a branch high above my head.

I take a deep breath, tuck the slipper into my pocket, then climb the tree, pressing the soles of my sore feet to the trunk so I can push myself up to the first branch. I keep climbing, until I reach the swallow, then stop and sit amongst the leaves in the moonlight. The little bird pecks at the crevice in between two branches. I unclasp my pendant from around my neck and place it into the nook of the branch. There is a dip in it deep enough to hold the pendant and the chain.

"Please look after it." I press my palm against the bark, and the willow sighs. The swallow flitters off, changing shape until it is nothing more than tendrils of blue magic again.

I sit in the tree for a while, cradling the glass slipper in my hands, and wonder why it didn't disappear with my dress when the magic wore off. I'm too tired to think of an explanation. I'm just glad to have something left of the magical night I had with Ash.

By the time I climb down and make my way home to my cottage, it's almost sunrise. I hide the glass slipper in my blanket box, then fall onto my bed and close my eyes, hoping sleep will come quickly. I drift for an unknown amount of time, aware of the birds chirping outside, but stuck in the half-way place between wakefulness and sleep.

Something bangs.

"Ella," Anna's shrill voice shouts. "Come out right now."

I roll over and curl into a ball, then pull the blanket up and put my arms over my head, in no mood to deal with my horrible stepsister. If she's here, it means I missed breakfast. Right now, I don't care. They can look after themselves for one day.

"Ella," Drew says this time. "You better open the door."

"Now, girl," Lady Roche demands.

More banging.

I sit up. Lady Roche never comes to my cottage.

I *am* in trouble.

I push my matted hair away from my face, and get out of bed. The door sticks like it always does, and I have to lift it to open it. Lady Roche stands on the other side of the threshold, flanked by my two stepsisters. They don't look very impressed.

"My gosh, you look terrible," Anna says.

"You better get cleaned up," Lady Roche adds.

Drew scowls. "You have a visitor."

The girls step aside. Ash is standing a way up the path that leads to the front door of my cottage. He holds the reins of a beautiful black horse in one hand, in the other is something wrapped in silk. A carriage pulled by two more horses sits behind him. Ash rocks on his heels, a smile curling his lips upwards.

I haven't washed or changed since before the ball. I look down at my grubby, torn clothes. At the dirt on my hands and feet. I really must be a sight.

"Thank you, Lady Roche," Ash says, leading the horse towards us. "Perhaps you can go up to Roche Manor now? My parents will be arriving soon."

Lady Roche hitches her skirt and raises her chin. She doesn't reply, but turns and walks past Ash. My stepsisters follow.

"My carriage will take you back," Ash says. "Eleanor and I will be along shortly. I trust you will have tea ready when we arrive."

"As you wish," Lady Roche says, but her pursed lips suggest she is far from happy about taking orders from Ashwin Chethan.

Ash's driver opens the carriage door for Lady Roche and my stepsisters, and they pile in. Ash watches them drive up the forest road before turning back to me.

I have so many things I want to say to him. How I'm sorry for running away. That I wish the night had ended differently. How I should have told him the truth about who I am. But the words are stuck in my mouth, and all I can do is stare at him.

"I brought you something."

"A horse?" I cross the threshold and walk to ash, holding my hand out to stroke the animal's nose.

"And this." He holds out the silk-wrapped parcel.

I curl my fingers around it, feeling the solid item underneath the smooth fabric, but I don't unwrap it.

"Why are you here?" I finally manage to ask.

"Because I want to be."

"But … you know who I am now." I stare down at the silk in my hands. It's blue, like my gown was. "You shouldn't be here."

"Why?" Ash reaches out and lifts my chin with his finger. "Because you're treated like a servant?"

"I am a servant."

Ash shakes his head. "Even if you are, I don't care. Now open this, or I will." He puts his hand over mine holding the parcel.

I fold back the silk to reveal the glass slipper I lost running down the steps of Chethan Manor. It glitters, and I smile.

"Thank you. The slippers are all I have left from last night."

"You have more than just a pair of shoes." Ash takes my hand and squeezes it gently. "You have me. And this horse."

I frown and look from Ash to the beautiful mare, and back again. "What do you mean?"

Ash shrugs. "I assumed she had something to do with the spell you cast. She isn't one of ours, and I found her roaming the grounds shortly after you ran off."

"I did wonder why my slippers didn't disappear." I look down at the shoe in my hand. "I have the other one inside."

"Maybe we don't need an explanation."

ELLA AND ASH

Bird song fills the air, and a swallow lands between the horse's ears.

"Maybe." I stare at the horse and her bird companion, remembering back to when her partner and my driver returned to swallows, and the carriage disintegrated. To when ash used the Bain pocket watch. Did stopping time have something to do with it? "Everyone was frozen, and I still had my shoes."

"What are you talking about?" Ash asks.

I look at him, excited. "You stopped time. Maybe you stopped it before my spell wore off completely."

"Or maybe the willow tree wanted you to have something special."

The swallow chirps a few notes before taking to the air and fluttering off. The black mare whinnies and tosses her head, then nuzzles my cheek with her velvety nose. Ash and I laugh.

"A gift from my mother, perhaps. Does she have a name?"

"I'm sure you can give her one."

"Swallow."

"Perfect," Ash says. "Come on. My parents are eager to meet you."

"But I'm a mess. I can't greet them looking like this."

"You're beautiful no matter what."

I frown. "I'm covered in dirt. At least let me wash and change."

"Okay. I'll wait out here." Ash lets go of my hand, and leads Swallow up the path.

Inside, I tuck the glass slipper away with its pair in my blanket box, then quickly freshen up and change. A brush won't tame my messy hair, so I twist it up into a bun. I spray my wrists and neck with rosewater, slip my shoes on, then tug the door closed and walk to where Ash stands with Swallow.

"Do you want to ride her?" he asks, handing me the reins.

I grip the leather straps. "She's bareback."

"It's not a problem." Ash taps her front leg, and the horse kneels. He climbs on, and Swallow stands again. "Your turn." Ash holds his hand out to me.

I take it, and he gently pulls me up onto Swallow's back so I'm seated behind him. We walk up the path towards Roche Manor, and I wrap my arms around Ash's waist, resting my cheek against his back. I concentrate on his warmth, and listen to the birds chirping in the trees.

"You may be surprised when we see your family," Ash says. "I had a little chat with them earlier."

"Oh." I lift my head. "What about?"

"I came to the house this morning looking for you. When they said you hadn't showed up for breakfast, I asked them a few questions about how you're related to them." He pauses. "Let's just say, what they told me was *very* interesting."

"Are you going to tell me what they said? Or make me squirm?"

"I used my ring, so I think you already know what

they said."

I smile to myself. If Ash really did use his artefact on them, Lady Roche would have told him that I have as much claim to Roche Manor as she does, if not more.

When we reach the house, Ash slides off Swallow then helps me down. Phillip holds the door open for us. Since my mother died, no one in this house has ever held the door open for me. We step through into the parlour. Lady Roche, my stepsisters, and Ash's parents are seated around a table spread with tea and scones. It seems my family has done as Ash asked.

Lord Chethan stands to greet us. I hang back, positive he has stood for his son and not for me.

"Is this the girl you wish us to meet?" he asks.

"Yes, Father," Ash says. "This is Eleanor. She was at the ball last night."

I stand with my hands clasped in front of me, and stare at my feet. There is no way Lord and Lady Chethan will approve of me.

"Young lady, look at me," Lord Chethan says.

I raise my head, and I'm surprised to see him smiling.

"Is it true this is your father's house?" Lady Chethan asks, coming to her husband's side.

"Yes, my lady, it is." I grip the fingers of my left hand tightly with my right, resisting the urge to curtsey even though I should. I'm not sure why I choose this exact moment to be rebellious.

"That would mean it is also your house," Lord Chethan

says. "Presumably." He glances at Lady Roche, and she quickly averts her gaze.

"What is my father's is also mine," I say. "My mother passed away three years ago."

Lord Chethan frowns. "I'm sorry for your loss."

"And I for yours." I offer him a sad smile.

"Father? Can we get to what we talked about?" Ash raises his eyebrows.

"Ah, yes." Lord Chethan stands with his hands behind his back, then rocks on his feet like I've seen Ash do so many times. "It seems Lady Roche has been mistreating you, Eleanor."

I don't reply. I just wait for him to continue.

"She has made you her servant?" Lady Chethan asks. "In your own home?"

I take a deep breath, and stare at my feet again. "That seems to be what's happened. Yes."

"This is madness." Drew jumps to her feet and stamps her foot. "This is our house."

"Be quiet, child," Lord Chethan says.

Anna rises from her chair and comes to stand beside Ash. "Ella's father married our mother, so that makes Roche Manor ours." She turns to Ash. "I'm sure you would rather be seen with someone like me on your arm, than someone like *her*."

I look up at Anna's remark, shocked that she is being so rude in front of Lord and Lady Chethan. Ash looks at her in a peculiar way, and then I notice the tiara Anna is wearing. She's trying to make Ash fall in love with her. I close my eyes for a moment, because I've seen how the tiara works. My father is under its spell.

Ash has no hope of resisting it.

Lord Chethan chuckles. "You silly girl. Your artefact won't work on my son."

Ash takes Anna's hand. Her eyes light up and she gives Lord Chethan a look that suggests she knows better.

"Anna?" Ash says. "Do you really love me?"

My heart sinks at his words, because of course she is going to say yes. It seems he is in her thrall after all.

"Of course not," Anna blurts. "I just want your money."

My stepsister gasps, and pulls her hand from Ash's, covering her open mouth.

Ash smirks at her. "It seems my artefact is more powerful than yours. And the truth always prevails."

11

I wave my hand, and the dirty plates on the kitchen table stack themselves. With another flick of my wrist, they fly to the sink and land in the soapy water.

"Would you like anything else for lunch?" Anna asks. "Before I clear the table?"

"No, thank you," I reply. "I'm off to the cemetery."

Anna smiles then waves her hand, and the leftover food is packed away in the pantry and the meat safe.

"Oh, you didn't leave anything for me to do," Drew says.

"You can wipe the table." Anna floats a dishcloth over to Drew, and she sets to work cleaning up the crumbs.

Since Lord and Lady Chethan came to see us after

the masquerade ball, things have been a little different around Roche Manor. My stepsisters are actually behaving like civil human beings, and Lady Roche has allowed me to use magic in the house again. Which means I'm no longer a servant, and at my request, we haven't hired one.

I suggested we all pitch in to help around the place, so it seems I'm now considered an equal to my stepsisters. I guess people will do anything under the threat of losing all their magical possessions. Lord Chethan practically ordered Lady Roche to treat me as she would her own daughters.

And the next time my father comes home, she is to tell him what she did.

I'm not yet sure if that's a good or a bad thing. We will have to wait and see.

But I now have my own room in the manor. We converted the attic into a bedroom, and I'm finally making use of all the wonderful things my mother left me.

"Have fun," Anna says.

"And say hi to Ash." Drew looks up from the table where the dishcloth is moving back and forth on its own.

I smile to myself as I leave the house. I'm not stupid. I know Anna and Drew are very good at acting. It's actually fun watching them catch themselves when they're about to fall back into their previously horrid ways.

The sun warms my skin as I walk across the grounds of Roche Manor towards the stables. Ash said he would come and collect me today, but I told him I wanted to ride Swallow. Gerald has Swallow saddled for me, and I ride to the road to meet Ash.

"Are you ready?" he asks.

I nod, and Ash climbs up onto Swallow's back behind me. We rock gently as she walks us to the cemetery, and I lean back into Ash's chest. At the gate, we tether Swallow to a post then go in.

The climb up the hill to my mother's grave is different today. It's the first time Ash and I have done it together. I'm not sure what to expect. I have no idea why I think anything will have changed in the past week. But I'm hoping the tree will allow me to take my pendant back. Until now, I haven't wanted to ask for it.

When we reach the top of the hill I go immediately to my mother's headstone and kneel on the grass. I run my finger over the golden words etched into the rock.

"Hi, Mother, how are you?" I ask. "There's someone I'd like you to meet."

Ash has been here several times already, and although I've talked about him, I've never actually introduced him to my mother.

He steps forward, and in a hesitant voice he says, "Hi, Lady Adaline. I'm Ashwin."

The leaves of the willow tree stir as a gentle breeze wafts through. My heart fills with happiness, because I can feel the loving sigh of the tree pulsing through the air and the earth.

I get to my feet and take Ash's hand. "Come on."

We walk into the shade of the willow's branches, and I stand at the trunk with my hand pressed against it, like I have so many times before. I have cried so many tears of sadness under this tree, and it's a relief this time when my tears come, because they are tears of joy.

Joy for a better future.

And for finding someone special in Ashwin Chethan.

My tears fall to the dirt, and the familiar blue glow seeps into the tree. It snakes its way up the trunk and into the branches, lighting up every leaf, making the tree grow. I kick off my shoes and shimmy up the trunk to the first branch, then look down at Ash.

"You coming?" I ask.

He smiles up at me and kicks off his own shoes. Seconds later, he is perched on the branch beside me.

"Lead the way." Ash kisses me quickly on the temple.

I giggle and climb the tree, all the way to the top, and find the crevice where I hid my pendant. I look inside at the softly pulsing glow of the blue stone. I try to reach it, but my hand is too big to fit in the nook.

"We might need some help to get it out." I sit on the branch and let my legs swing.

Ash sits beside me. "How do we do that?"

I twirl my finger and create a tendril of magic, letting it float down into the tree's leaves. It swirls around itself, creating my magic swallow. The bird chirps, flittering up to land on my knee.

"Could you please retrieve my pendant?" I ask the

ELLA and ASH

little bird.

It takes flight towards the crevice, turning to smoke the moment before it passes through the small crack. Seconds later, the smoke emerges and reforms into the swallow, the chain of my pendant held firmly in its beak. The magical bird hovers in front of me, then drops the artefact onto my palm.

"Thank you," I say, releasing the bird.

It flies down into the tree, bursting into a flash of blue light before the magic seeps back into the leaves.

"Here, let me." Ash takes my pendant and undoes the clasp, then fastens it around my neck.

He moves his hands to my shoulders and stares into my eyes. I hold his gaze, happy in this moment where we don't need words to say how we feel. Ash knows me in a way I never thought anyone could. It's as though he can see into my heart and my soul.

"Thank you," I say.

"What for?" He runs his thumb over my cheek.

"For not letting my *standing* come between us." I grin, and Ash chuckles.

"Nothing will ever come between us. Eleanor, my princess."

He leans in, and presses his lips softly to mine. I wrap my arms around his neck, and when I fall, Ash is there to catch me.

THANK YOU

Thank you for taking the time to read *Ella and Ash*. As an indie author, I rely on reviews and word of mouth to help promote my books. Please consider posting a review at your place of purchase. If you would like to personally let me know what you think, you can email me at kalast@kalastbooks.com.au.

ABOUT THE AUTHOR

K. A. Last has always been artistic and creative. She has a diploma in Graphic Design and has worked in the publishing industry for more than twenty years. Blessed with a vivid imagination, she began writing to let off creative steam and fell in love with it. She also has a Bachelor of Arts degree from Charles Sturt University with a major in English, and minors in Children's Literature, Art History, and Visual Culture. She resides in the Australian countryside with her family and a menagerie of animals.

CONNECT WITH K. A. LAST

Website www.kalastbooks.com.au
Facebook www.facebook.com/KALastBooks
Instagram www.instagram.com/kalastbooks
Goodreads www.goodreads.com/KALast
Amazon www.amazon.com/author/kalast

Scan the code
to subscribe to
K. A. Last's
newsletter.